Aine MacTavish wasn't surprised to find herself at a bar in the wee hours of the morning, paying her father's tab, and escorting him back home. Again. She had to admit, though, she really wasn't expecting the spaceship they ran into on the way or the lizard-looking aliens who tossed her into a small cell and informed her that she would soon be auctioned to the highest bidder as a pleasure-giver. She was even more shocked to see all the other stolen females from around the galaxy who were facing the same fate as her.

After two years of captivity, Grizolde Theodosius Ja"Lento, warrior and cousin to the kind of Tarilax, had lost all hope of regaining his freedom or his lost honor. There was no way he could return to his homeland now, a broken and disgraced slave. That is, until the Lizentine tyrant, Beahl, abducts a beautiful Earther female with hair the color of red Packari sands and soft, warm eyes that remind him of the stormy azure seas of home. *Mine.*

For her, he would break the chains of captivity and restore his honor. For his mate, he would risk everything to make himself worthy.

His Warrior Princess
Copyright © 2021 D. Morrissey
ISBN: 978-1-4874-3293-5
Cover art by Martine Jardin

Published by eXtasy Books Inc

Look for us online at:
www.eXtasybooks.com

# His Warrior Princess
# Tarilean Adventures 2

## By

## D. Morrissey

# CHAPTER ONE

Aine

"When in Rome, the tough get going," Bruce drawls reverting to his thick Scottish brogue.

After living here in the States for more than twenty years, he only does it when he's drunk or nervous.

"Do as the Romans," I correct him as per our usual repartee.

"What?"

Sighing, I hand the bartender my credit card and give her an exasperated look before returning my attention to Bruce. "When in Rome, do as the Romans."

"Aye, lass. That's what I said," he argues, then slams a shot of Glendronach and bangs the empty glass on the bar.

"He's cute," the bartender says to me, smiling and eyeing Bruce like a slice of chocolate cake before she takes off to the other end of the bar with my card.

If she only knew. First of all, that's my father she's ogling so blatantly. Secondly, that's just *ew*. Lastly, he was only cute the first dozen or so times. This is the third time this week alone that I've had to fetch him home from a bar and pay off his tab. We are way beyond cute now.

"She thinks I'm braw," he says, waggling his brows and somehow managing to slur a whisper. "She's quite the bonny thing, too. Maybe you should go home and leave your old man here for a wee bit longer? Run along, and I'll see you back at the hoose in the mornin'?"

"In your dreams, Romeo. You're coming home with me."

"Here you go, hon." The young bartender hands me my card, and I stand up, stowing it away in my back pocket. "Your friend here is a trip. I hope you guys come back," she says, winking at my father.

"I'm sure he will. In fact, I doubt I'll be able to stop him." Irritation drips from my tone, my look sharp onto him. "But, for now, I'm taking my *friend* home so he can sleep it off. C'mon, Bruce. Let's go."

Upon a sharp tug on his arm, he stands up reluctantly.

"Careful there, lass. All you have to do is ask. You catch more flies with worms, you know."

"Honey," I correct him again without even thinking about it, catching him under the arm as he stumbles between the barstools.

"What, sugar?"

I blow out an aggravated breath as the bartender chuckles behind us. Any other day, I might have found humor in this, but not today. I'm tired. Bone weary, as some say.

"I wasn't calling you honey. It's 'you catch more flies with honey.' You're mixing it up with 'the early bird gets the worm.' Now, can you walk out of here by yourself? Or do we need to carry you?"

I sincerely hope he can walk since one, the bar is nearly empty and I don't see anyone who might be able to help, and two, I don't have a vehicle to carry him to.

He gives me an incredulous look and puffs out his chest. "Of course I can walk. I was walking long before you were even a glimmer in your blessed mother's eye, as you weel-ken."

"Yes, yes. I know. I'm sorry."

What I really know is that he goes through several different stages emotionally when he's shit-faced, sometimes getting a bit surly when his drinking is interrupted. The last thing I want is to spend the night dealing with my obstinate father when I have to get up early in the morning and go to work. He, on the other hand, can lie-in and sleep it off since he's still unemployed after the last electric company where he worked went belly-up some months ago. Best to just go along with everything he says and keep him appeased so he'll skip straight to the melancholy part of our evening.

"See you later." The bartender waves at us with her little white towel, and I nod my thanks while tossing a little wave behind us.

"Speaking of your blessed mother—" he says as we make our way to the exit.

Those words always make me cringe. If he gets started talking about my mum, there's a good chance we'll be up all night until he cries himself to sleep in the wee hours of the morning.

"Pop," I interrupt, trying to sidetrack him. "We're going to have to walk back to the house. I couldn't get the truck to start."

"That twally-washer piece of shite," he mumbles. "Hey. How about I go back over there, and have that nice bartender lass call us a cab?"

I open the door and give him a skeptical look, unsure whether he's actually wanting a cab, another drink, or the bartender's phone number. Whatever. It doesn't matter, because it's not going to happen, especially the cab. I'm tapped out after paying his tab, and we've barely got enough cash left for groceries to hold us over until my next payday. Cabs are definitely a luxury we can't afford right now.

"How about we just walk instead? It's a nice night, and we can talk."

"Talk? Since when do you ever want to talk?"

He steps outside, and I follow him, the door swishing shut behind us.

He's got a point. I've never been much of a talker. Took

after my mum in that respect.

"Just humor me. I've been stuck in a tiny cubicle inside a noisy office all day, and a little bit of fresh air will do me good. Let's cut through there. It's faster."

I point to the woods on the other side of the bar's parking lot, hoping it truly is a shortcut. Honestly, I have no idea whether it's shorter or not, but it has to be safer than stumbling down the side of the road at two in the morning. The last thing I need is to get mugged or raped, and my Hello Kitty nightshirt just screams "easy target."

"Och aye the noo!" Bruce bellows out of nowhere and stumbles off in the direction of the woods with me hot on his heels. "We best get crackin' then, lassie."

I glance around nervously, just to make sure no would-be robbers or ninja assassins are watching, and then follow him into the woods. Luckily, there's a full moon lighting the path and making it easier to see. I put on a little speed so I can get in front of Bruce. No telling where he'd lead us.

"Let's stay together," I suggest while looping my arm through his. "The last thing we need is to get separated out here. I might never find you again."

"Don't worry, lass. I'd find you. I'm part Scottish bloodhound, you ken. I could find a skelf in an iron outhouse."

Much to my irritation, I giggle at his thick, familiar brogue. Lord knows, he doesn't need any encouragement, so I stifle it quickly. "Well, stay close to me, anyway. It's dark and spooky out here, and I'm scared."

"Aine, you've got the blood of the Bruce in you. You ain't never been scared of nothing or no one, and I'm sure it'd take more than a full moon and a few overgrown trees to have you shivering in your long skirts."

"Oh, Bruce. If only that were true. I've been scared plenty," I confess.

It's true. I've been scared plenty of times. For instance, I was petrified when my mother died of cancer a few years ago and left me alone to take care of Pop and my big brother, Lachlin. I was terrified when Lachlin disappeared last year without a word or a single trace. And, more than anything else, I'm frightened beyond words every day that my father won't be there when I get home from my crummy, dead-end job at the call center. He's all I have left. Well, that, and the hope that someday, we'll find Lachlin.

Bruce places his hand on my shoulder and gives it a reassuring squeeze. "But you have the strength and courage of a Scottish warrior, Ainie. Your mum, God rest her soul, was a direct descendent of the great William Wallace. They didn't come any braver than your mum. Between her blood and mine, you were born to lead revolutions, my dear."

I roll my eyes. I've heard this nonsense — or havering, if you're Scottish — all my life. At twenty-one, the only revolution I've ever led is the one at work when we ran out of coffee in the break room.

"Just remember," he says, all serious-like and barely slurring. "Without fear, there's no such thing as courage."

That might be true, but right now, I can feel all my courage seeping out through the soles of my shoes as garish moonlight trickles in through the gnarly branches of the thick copse and casts a creepy pallor on the pathway. I wish now that we'd taken our chances with the sidewalks and the city streets.

"Maybe." I rest my head against his broad arm as we walk. "But, sometimes, I'm just a little girl who wants her pop."

"You're a good girl, Aine MacTavish." He smiles and pats my hand. "Your mum would be proud."

I nearly tear up at the sentiment, but then, I remember he's trashed and probably won't even remember what he said tomorrow. We've apparently reached the nostalgic and affectionate stage of the evening ahead of schedule.

Before I know it, we pop out of the woods into the middle

of a large, sleepy meadow about the size of a football field, with tall oaks surrounding us on all sides. It might actually be a pretty place in the daylight, but something about it gives me the heebie-jeebies right now.

A little tingle runs up my spine — the feeling there's eyes on us. I shiver and huddle closer to Bruce, glancing behind us at the path that disappears back into the dark, dense woods. We're too far in now to turn around and go back. So, I take a deep breath and give my pop's arm a tug while dragging us toward the other side, continuously scanning the tree line around us. Surely, I'm just being paranoid.

"Slow down, there, lass. It's no foot race we're running here."

Bruce huffs as he unwinds my arm from his, looking around while he takes in a few deep breaths. I hadn't realized how fast I'd been walking.

"Sorry, Bruce. I just need to get us home so we can eat something and go to bed. I have to be at work early tomorrow." I don't want to admit that this place has me spooked, and has me wanting to get the hell out of here as fast as we can.

"Aye. You need your sleep, I ken. I shouldn'a went out to-night, but I was feeling restless and didn'a ken what to do with myself. I'm sorry, pet."

Movement ahead catches my eye, making me gasp in spite of myself. The hair on the back of my neck begins to crawl up my scalp as a dark shadow creeps slowly and ominously across the field straight toward us.

I want to grab Bruce and run, but I must be terror-stricken because my legs are totally locked. All I can do is stare, confused and more than a little horrified. Before I know it, the shadow overtakes us, casting us in opaque darkness until I can barely see my hand in front of my face.

"What the—" Tipping my head upward, I'm suddenly

struck by a bright, blinding light, followed immediately by an invisible pressure that appears to be trying to squeeze my innards out through my belly button.

My eyes water, my ears pop and my lungs basically seize, making it hard to draw a full breath. I can't even move a muscle. Whatever this is, it has my feet rooted to the ground and my hands glued to my sides.

"Pop!" I shout, my voice stolen by sudden violent winds.

"Can you run, Aine?"

"No. I can't move." I'm trying to shake my head and struggling desperately against the invisible force.

"Let her go, you alien dobbers!"

*Alien?* I'm too freaked out to dwell on his word choice, focusing instead on trying to move my arms.

Ready to give up, I hear Bruce grunt then watch as he doubles over in pain. Moaning curses all the way, he finally slumps to the ground in a heap.

"Stop it!" I scream, tears flooding my cheeks now. "Leave him alone! You're killing him!"

I don't know if he's dead or not, but it only adds to my hysteria. I scream until my throat is raw and I'm dizzy from lack of oxygen.

"Don't. Hurt. My—" I rasp at last, feeling my legs give out and the darkness begin to seep in before I can even finish the sentence.

*Father* is my last thought before the shadow totally consumes me.

# CHAPTER TWO

Griz

"Just the female. Leave the male," Beahl orders as his ruthless watchdog opens the hatch.

I hate this. Every cell in my body revolts, and I want to kill him where he stands. It would be so easy, but my hands are tied. All I can do is try my best to help the poor female as we go along.

I pause at the top of the stairs, trying to figure out the best way to do that. It's bad enough that we're ripping the little female away from her home world and everything that she knows, only to sell her on the intergalactic black market as a pleasure giver. Maybe having a familiar presence with her will be of some small consolation. I could, at least, do that much for the poor creature.

"Your call." I'm trying to sound as flippant as possible. "It's just the male looks to be in fairly good shape. You could probably sell him for a tidy sum as a field hand or a house servant."

Beahl's forehead furrows, and his long, bony fingers tug at his thin, black lips. The action brings out more of his human-oid features, which are usually secondary to his reptilian genome.

"Perhaps you're right, but I've never actually recovered a male before."

"Um . . ." I tap my chest not so subtly. "I'm not sure that's entirely true. Besides, male or female. What's the difference?"

Beahl smirks, amused. "If you don't know the difference by now, Griz, you're a bigger froekhead than I thought you were."

I snarl at him, unable to do much more. Someday, I will take great pleasure in slowly plucking every limb from his foul body, just before I rip off his ugly head. Unfortunately, it won't be today, not while he has my dam and not while I still have this frizzucking slave implant embedded against my skull.

"You know what I mean," I snap. "The cells and the cuffs don't differentiate between femkis and mackis. Trapped is trapped, and a slave is a slave. Both can be sold at market."

Beahl looks at me suspiciously now. Wokshite! I should have kept my mouth shut. He knows I would never help him willingly. What was I thinking?

"I don't know what game you're playing at, Tarilean. Yet. But you can be sure that I'll figure it out. Still, you may be right. We'll bring them both for now, and if he turns out to be useless, I'll just shove him through the airlock." He chuckles. "I'll send Lionese to help carry them up."

I nod, managing one step down the stairs before he stops me again.

"Oh, and Griz," he purrs.

With a raised brow, I turn to face him.

"I didn't actually recover you, remember? You were *gifted* to me by the Goridians," he reminds me. "A tribute, you could say."

Like I could forget. How could anyone forget the kind of pain, torture and humiliation they put me through? Me, Grizolde Theodosius Ja'Lento, warrior and cousin to the king of Tarilax, reduced to slavery, all because of this stupid implant.

No doubt my people believe me dead, which is probably for the best at this point. I'd be too ashamed to ever face them again, anyway, even if I did escape. *When* I escape, rather, because I will escape. I will have my revenge. Those accursed Goridian pirates are a scourge on the universe and must be eradicated. They are next on my list, just as soon as I take care of Beahl and his crew of honor-less miscreants.

I curl my lip at him and then turn away to retrieve the new slaves.

The ground feels strange beneath my feet, damp and almost spongy, and it takes a minute to get used to the unusual pull of the gravity and the rich, oxygenated air. It's been many cycles since we've docked anywhere, and I've grown accustomed to the weightlessness of space and the dingy, metal surroundings of the ship. Out here, the world seems boundless and beautiful, and the urge to run is almost overwhelming, though I know I can't. Not and live, anyway.

Pushing the urge way down deep, I look around, trying to absorb as much of the comely landscape as possible. So, this is Earth. I've never been here before and abhor the fact that my first visit is not a friendly one. Instead, I'm forced to help this scum steal a human female. A very precious, much sought-after human female, but still.

For some reason, everyone wants a human female these days. I hear my cousin even mated one. I've never seen a human, but I hear they're more precious than rare gems from a Drakon's treasury. Fortunately, the ones in captivity are usually treated well enough. After all, who would spend an entire fortune to own one, and then risk any damage to it? Personally, I wouldn't have one, not that I'd own a slave, anyway, even if I wasn't one myself. But, from what I've heard, they're weak and frail, and they don't live long enough for consumers to even recover their investments. I just don't get it.

Forcing my legs to move, I head toward the pair of humans who are both lying unconscious only a few feet away, and begin a quick examination. The male captures my attention first, as he's lying on his back face-up. It's almost a shock when I see how similar he is to my own appearance.

He appears to be middle-aged with a mop of thick dark hair, long enough that it partially covers his face. A light peppering of grey begins at his temples, giving him an air of maturity. He's dressed in strange-looking clothes and reeks strongly of methane or some other related toxin. Still, he looks healthy enough overall, albeit a bit on the puny side when compared to a Tarilean. In fact, he's much smaller than I initially thought, even. Definitely too small for a field hand, but he might do for a house slave.

Turning my attention to the female now, the first thing I notice is how tiny she is. Much smaller than the male, even, and she looks dainty and fragile. Passed out on her stomach, I can't see her face, but she appears to be a youngling. Beahl has made a mistake. Not even he can sell a youngling as a pleasure giver, and the auction house won't pay as much for a house servant. I reach out and gently roll her over.

Holy frizzuck! She is definitely no youngling. Of that, I'm certain. My cock agrees, erasing any doubt as it stiffens almost painfully against the scratchy fabric of my pants. Her hair is the color of a Tarilean sunset, long and red with hints of honey and gold as it fans out around her angelic face. The unique color serves to highlight her soft, pale skin and delicate features. Her full, luscious lips seem to call to mine, begging to be kissed and nipped. Mouth watering and pulse quickening, my eyes dip lower, taking in her nubile curves, which are enough to tempt a Symlian saint.

*Mine! My mate!*

My breath hitches and I jerk my hands away, staring at the tempting little female. Where the haelic had that come from? Something deep inside, something ancient and nearly forgotten, had demanded it.

My hearts expand, and there's a sharp pain as I think about what he's going to do with her. The little pixie is too beautiful for words, and I couldn't bear to see her come to harm. I can't even seem to tear my eyes away from her. My instincts revolt, overwhelmed with the need to protect her.

While reaching a trembling hand to stroke her lovely face, a red-hot streak of pure lust flashes up my arm through my fingertips, flooding my veins with molten lava. I jolt and jerk my hand away, shocked by my body's reaction.

"I'll get this one." A deep, gravelly voice brings me back to the moment rather harshly. "Or, we can trade, and I'll carry that one. It looks lighter, anyway."

My breath hisses out of me, and my hands clench into fists. I'll be damned if this dirty Lizentine slaver lays a finger on my mate!

Wait. Mate? No!

My shoulders sag, and I stare down at the sweet face of the helpless little femki sleeping so peacefully before me. *Mate,* my body and my instincts insist.

Please, goddess, not now, and not with a human, especially not this human who I am virtually powerless to protect.

I know it's true, though. I can literally feel the answer in my gut, stronger than a hunch, even more driving than a thousand year-old intuit. This is my *amavi compar,* my fated mate. My hearts know it, my body knows it, and my brain is slowly grasping the concept. She's mine, and there's not a frizzucking thing I can do about it.

"C'mon. We don't have all night," Lionese says as he grasps the male's collar and starts dragging him toward the ship.

Panic sets in, and my eyes dart around like frightened fireflies searching for a way out of this. If I pick her up and run, he'll just set off the explosive device in my head and take her, anyway, once I'm dead. Then, she'd have no one at all to look out for her.

If I stay alive, I can at least help keep her safe until we get to Janyx. And, there's my dam to think about.

If only this beauty in my arms were awake, I could make her run. I give her a little shake out of desperation, knowing it will be hours before she recovers from the effects of the impactor.

"Amavi, wake up. Please, wake up," I beg, but she doesn't move, her face still relaxed in slumber, and her breaths steady.

"Griz!"

I look up to see Lionese waiting for me at the top of the stairs.

"Coming," I reply, resigned and defeated. I have already failed. I cannot even keep my mate safe. Tucking my hands beneath her, I lift her gently and head back to the ship.

My mate is like a feather in my arms, her scent a mix between the Haepler blooms and the Gossimer firs back home on Tarilax. It's a titillating blend of hope and nostalgia, and, apparently, a heady aphrodisiac. My cock is so hard it aches, which is very inconvenient at the moment with my hands full as I near the top of the stairs where Beahl is waiting impatiently.

"Look at her! She's magnificent!" He laughs as he drags a long, clawed finger softly down her rosy cheek.

Doing my best to stifle a growl, every instinct inside me urges me to wrap my fingers around his scaly, green throat and crush his larynx. Goddess help me, I can't stop myself from pulling her closer to me. Thankfully, Beahl doesn't seem to notice.

"Do you have any idea how much this female is worth?" He practically drools as he continues to caress her face. "We'll have to keep her separate from the others. I don't want anyone to damage her before we get there."

My entire body vibrates with rage at the very idea of anyone damaging her—blind, unmitigated anger that I cannot let loose or exercise without endangering both myself and my mate. By the fates! I will not survive this. It's too much. With-out a doubt, I will not be able to stop myself from killing an-yone who hurts her.

"I'll take her to Medical," I grit, trying desperately to get her away from him.

"Yes, do that. Tell Ceazare I want a language download, too, along with the usual implant."

I give a sharp nod in acknowledgement, not trusting my-self enough to speak.

"Hurry, now. I want to try and catch another one before we have to leave. Maybe we can get two or three more, as long as we're here?" he muses aloud as he slithers off toward the bridge.

I take a deep breath and adjust her in my arms, not because she's heavy, but because I want to feel her as close to my chest, to my hearts, as possible. Then, I head off down the winding passageway to the Med bay. Pausing one last time at the door, I sink my face into her soft, thick mane. Here in the dim hall-way, it looks dark, but I remember the glorious red and gold hues. I've never seen such a color before, and that, along with the texture and her scent, is enough to push me into a mating heat if I'm not careful.

For reasons I can't even explain, I lean forward and press my lips lightly to hers, lingering with my eyes closed while I bask in her delicious warmth. I've seen the soldiers and crew do the same thing to females during their raunchy mating frenzies. They call it *kissing*. It seemed an odd and barbaric practice to me over the years, and I've never had the urge to try it. Until now. I find I like it. Very much.

"Forgive me, *mis lustrava amavi compar*," I whisper, giving her hair one final nuzzle.

Sighing, I raise my head and push through the doors of the Med bay. Thank the goddess the healer is pure scientist through and through and doesn't seem to be quite as foul as

Beahl or Lionese, even though he, too, is Lizentine.

"Ah, Griz! There you are," Ceazare says as I lay my sleeping mate on the exam table.

Taking a moment to arrange her carefully, I continue hovering until he nudges me aside irritably. We both know I could crush him with one hand, but the implant keeps him safe from my temper.

"There, that's better. Now, let's see what we have here. Ooh, this is so exciting, Griz. Our first good look at this species."

"Yes," I reply, stowing my twitchy fingers as I step back to eye her more closely. By the fates! She's even more beautiful in the light.

Ceazare stands beside her holding a Med Reader Unit in his hand. With a flick of his wrist, the MRU comes to life, whirring softly as he begins the examination. Starting at her feet, he holds it a few inches above her, walking it slowly up her legs as he eyes the monitor. He pauses abruptly with the MRU hovering just above her hips, and then raises and lowers the device several times. His eyes narrow at the screen, and a little crinkle creases his forehead.

"Well, that's interesting," he murmurs.

"What? What's wrong with her?" My chest suddenly feels like a herd of floops are stampeding inside it. If someone has hurt my mate, I will come back for them. I will rip this planet apart and make them suffer.

"She must be younger than I thought. She is untouched."

"Untouched?"

"Yes. Definitely a virgin."

A virgin? Untouched? I let go of a breath that I hadn't realized I'd been holding.

"No, wait. She's no youngling. She's definitely fertile. See there?" He points to a green dot on the monitor, which means absolutely nothing to me.

Slowly, my eyes float shut, and I can't help but smile. My mate has saved herself for me, and I find this surprisingly satisfying.

"This will, no doubt, double her value at auction. A young, fertile human virgin? Unheard of! They'll all be fighting over her. Beahl will be very pleased."

At this, my eyes fly open, and a growl escapes from my throat. Over my dead body! I want to scream and rip him to pieces with my fangs, but I bite down on my tongue until the bitter, copper taste of blood floods my mouth.

"What's your problem?"

"Nothing," I snarl.

With great effort, I manage to control my anger while Ceazare finishes the exam.

"Everything looks good," he says, obviously pleased with my mate. "We just need to tag her, and we're done."

"Wait," I blurt, nearly forgetting Beahl's instructions. "Beahl says to give her a language download, too."

Ceazare cocks his brow at me. "Really? A language download?"

"I know. I was shocked, too. But that's what he said."

Language downloads are rare and quite expensive. Not many would consider giving one to a slave, so Ceazare's surprise is warranted. I've had mine for years, purchasing it for myself while I was on Elonia helping them fight for their independence against the Goridians.

Ceazare walks back to a row of cabinets behind the table and begins plundering through them. "I think I might have one in here somewhere. Oh! Here it is."

"Will it hurt her?" I ask, not really knowing if her fragile human body can withstand our technology.

Ceazare pauses, eyeing me cautiously. "What's wrong with you, Griz? You're about as nervous as a flisker in a room full of rockers."

Shiest! I need to chill. They cannot know that she is my mate. It would be dangerous for both of us. Frowning, I tap my fingers against my leg while I think. There's no question that if Ceazare is noticing a difference in my behavior, it won't take Beahl long at all to catch on.

"Nothing." I shrug dismissively. "She's just a tiny little thing, and I'd hate to see you damage her, is all. Beahl would come unhinged if anything happened to his human."

Ceazare nods, but I can tell he's not convinced as he clicks the download tube into a small pocket on the console behind us. He grabs one of the electrodes and places it behind her ear, pressing several buttons on the panel.

"Yes. He would, for sure. But, as you can see, she's fine and it's all done. Now, stop fidgeting and help me do the other implant. After that, you can strip her and dress her in more appropriate attire before you take her to her cell."

He points to a thin, silky beshaba folded neatly on the counter, dress typically only worn by pleasure slaves. Goddess help me, my cock bobs its approval.

As soon as Ceazare injects the slave implant beneath her scalp, Beahl's voice floats through the room from the overhead com. "Ceazare, come see me right away."

He sighs, peeling off his gloves and chucking them into the recycler.

"I'm sorry, Griz." He's pouting like a youngling who's just had their favorite toy taken away. "You'll have to finish this up yourself. Go ahead and strip her. Throw these rags in the trash after you dress her in the beshaba. When you're done, take her directly to solitaire and make sure she's locked up tight. I'm sure Beahl will want to take some extra safety precautions once he hears my findings."

"Yes," I croak, swallowing audibly. My mind stuck on the notion of stripping her, I barely register anything else he says. I step forward slowly and grip the hem of her tunic in my hand.

Once I'm sure Ceazare's gone and the door has shut firmly behind him, I begin tugging the strange garment over her head, only briefly wondering about the odd creature depicted on it. It looks almost like a felinian, but not quite. Then, my hearts racing and my pulse pounding an urgent tempo in my ears, I drag my hawkish gaze down the length of her.

My breath whooshes out in a rush, every drop of blood in my head racing straight to my cock at the sight of her pretty, pink nipples. My knees weaken, and I have to place my hands against the table to steady myself.

Gods, I'm in so much trouble.

# Chapter Three

Aine

"Ow." Still half-asleep, I reach my hand up and rub at the sore spot on my head. I must have bumped it last night in my sleep.

Not quite ready to get up, I roll back over on my side and snuggle into the pillow, an unfamiliar, and unpleasant, smell stirring my senses and making my nose crinkle. I suppose I'm off work today since I'm sleeping in, but everything seems kind of mixed up and fuzzy.

Wait. A. Minute.

My eyes pop open, and even though my vision is blurry, I know immediately that I'm not in my room. More than that, I know I'm not even in Arkansas anymore. Okay, then. Where the hell am I?

A light flickers overhead, and I struggle to make out the strange noises around me. *Shit!* I jackknife to a sitting position in the bed, flinging my legs over the side and blinking the morning goop out of my eyes. No. Not a bed. A cot. What the actual fuck?

Disoriented, I glance around at my surroundings, trying to swallow the onset of alarm as flashes of last night begin to rush back all at once. I need to get a hold of myself and calmly assess the situation. Panicking is not going to help anything.

Reaching deep, I find a tiny sliver of courage and hang on to it for dear life, forcing it to the forefront. I close my eyes and take a deep breath. Then, exhaling slowly, I stand up, open my eyes and take stock.

The room is small, and I'm on what I assume is some sort of transport. The hum of engines registers beneath my feet, and somehow, I just know that we're moving. I have no idea of the time, and there aren't any windows to provide me with clues. Even if there were, I have an eerie feeling that I'd only see darkness outside.

There's no bathroom in sight, but there's a toilet standing alone in the far corner with a box of stuff that might be tissue sitting next to it. Not even a sink to wash my hands. How nice.

Cutting my eyes to my skimpy wardrobe, I note that I'm barefooted, wearing some sort of weird dress made from a soft, silky material that hangs about mid-thigh. I can't tug it down any further without my boobs falling out of the top. The fabric criss-crosses over my breasts, leaving my back naked and wide open. Naturally, not a stitch of underwear.

And, oh, my god! There are bars stretching across the entire front wall of my room, revealing a grey, dead-end hallway on the other side.

No, not a room. A cell.

Maybe I should have noticed that first, that I was some kind of prisoner, but my mind is having a hard time processing everything. Suddenly, I remember Bruce, and my stomach lurches.

Pop! Had he been taken, too? Did they hurt him? Please let him have escaped. I move warily to the bars, testing them in my grip. As suspected, they're cold and impossibly strong. Iron, maybe?

A flurry of whispers and soft, feminine murmurs waft down the hallway from somewhere nearby, stirring a small splinter of hope inside me.

"He . . . Hello?" The sound dies abruptly, and I hear only silence once again. "Is anyone there? Talk to me. Please."

"See? She's alive," someone says.

"Be quiet," someone else replies.

"Hello?" I try again. "Where are you? Are you locked up, too?"

"Shh!" Someone hisses at me. "Do you want to bring the guards back here again?"

Guards?

"Who are you?" I try to talk lower this time, not wanting to agitate the only people around me who might have answers.

"Prisoners. Same as you," one of them tosses back.

"Prisoners? Whose prisoners? Where are we?"

Someone sighs heavily, and I can hear people shuffling around now.

"The aliens'. We're on their spaceship."

"They're taking us to sell as sex slaves," the other girl adds.

The wind knocks out of me, my heart jackhammering in my chest. "Sex slaves?"

"Why did you tell her that? She just woke up," the first girl snaps. "Couldn't you give her five minutes to process being abducted by aliens first?"

I turn around and lean my back against the cold, hard bars, gulping deep breaths and trying not to freak out. I've never hyperventilated in my life, but I suspect I'm on the verge of a major panic attack. I'm talking a doozy.

Abducted? By *aliens*? That's impossible. I want to laugh, but then, I remember Bruce's words from last night. *Alien dobbers*, he'd said.

"What's your name?" the softer voice asks, piercing through my little bubble of chaos and disbelief.

"Aine." My voice sounds small, even to me.

"Hi, Aine. I'm Jill, and this is Celia," she says, as if I can see them.

"Nice to meet you, Jill and Celia. How many of us are there?"

"Well, that depends on what you mean by *us*. Do you mean prisoners? Or, humans?"

"What?" My knees begin to buckle.

Jill takes a deep breath and exhales with a shaky puff. "We don't know for sure how many prisoners there are because we can't actually see past our cell. We can't ask because no one here can understand anyone else, except for me, you and Celia. From what I can tell, though, there could be at least fifty of us, probably more. There's ten . . . um . . . *girls* in this cell alone, and I think there's at least three more cells on the other side of ours. I tried to count at breakfast."

"So many," I whisper, more to myself than to anyone else. "What did you mean about there being only a few humans?"

"We appear to be in the minority here." She chuckles, pausing as if to figure out how to proceed. "There's only two of us in here, plus you, I think. I don't know if there are any more in the other cells for sure, but if there are, they're not talking. You are human, right?"

"Of course," I reply, considering the weight of her words. "But, if the others aren't human, what are they?"

"I have no idea. It's not like we can ask them."

Shaking my head, I close my eyes again. I can't even begin to process all of this right now. My brain is already in danger of short-circuiting as it is. "Jill, have you seen a man?"

"A man?"

"Sure, hon. We've seen lots of men," Celia scoffs.

"Well, I'm looking for one in particular. Tall, dark hair, stocky build, in his early forties. His name is Bruce. He was with me last night."

"You can probably forget about him, sweetheart," Celia, the not so nice one, jeers. "Bruce is long gone by now."

"Shut up, Celia," Jill snaps.

"Stop coddling her. We're jammed in here like a bunch of sardines with all these fish-face, Wookie-looking fuckers.

And, she's over there like some fairytale princess with a nice, cozy cell all to herself. I bet she even has a bed. Don't you, Princess?"

For some reason, I don't want them to know the truth. I'm embarrassed by what seems to be preferential treatment, which I don't understand at all. Regardless, I want to fit in with my fellow prisoners, and I'd gladly give up the privacy of my own cell to be closer to them. I want them to like me. I need them to like me. Maybe, if we all work together, we can get out of here.

"No, I don't have a bed," I tell her, which is not a total lie. A cot is not a bed, exactly.

"Why do you have your own cell?"

Good question. I try to think, but all reason flies right out of my head. "I honestly have no idea."

"Right," Celia taunts. "You probably blew one of the guards."

"Celia!" Jill shouts, outraged on my behalf. "How can you be such a bitch? You should apologize."

"Apologize? For what? The truth? I will not. How else did she get set up with luxury accommodations? It's obvious that it's every woman for herself in here."

What's obvious to me is that Celia is a crazy bitch, and we'll never be a team. Without that, I'm not sure there's any way of getting out of here. Besides, luxury accommodations? Seriously? I look around at the sparse cell and sigh.

"I'm sorry, Aine. I think everyone's just angry and out of sorts right now. We've only been awake a few hours ourselves."

"That's understandable," I offer, determined to be the bigger person.

Keys clanging against metal echo down the corridor, and a cacophony of gasps and guttural moans breaks out from the cell next-door.

"Shh! Get back and be quiet," Jill warns. "It's the guards."

I get the impression from the fear emanating from their cell that the guards are not nice people, if they're even people at all.

A door at the end of the hall creaks open and then clangs shut with such finality, it makes me flinch. The only thing I can hear over the sound of blood rushing in my ears is a cart or a gurney wheeling its way slowly down the hall toward us. One by one, cell doors open and close, and the clatter of dishes and silverware fills the corridor.

A few of the girls next door sigh and let out nervous breaths, and I figure whoever this is, it's not the guards they initially feared. Before long, my mouth begins to water as the delicious aroma of herbs and roasted meat envelops me. At least, we're being well-fed.

"Holy shit. Well, hello there, sexy. Who might you be?"

Celia's velvety voice purrs next door, and my eyebrows jerk up to my hairline. So, a bitch and a slut. Good to know.

"I cannot believe you said that," Jill remarks, her disgust and embarrassment apparent.

"What? It's not like he can understand me. None of these idiots speak English."

"You never know," Jill replies. "Here, I'll take that. Thank you."

I assume she's speaking to Mr. Sex-on-a-Stick over there.

"Yeah. Thanks, hon. You're a lot nicer to look at than that robot with a twat that brought our breakfast this morning," Celia mumbles around a mouthful of food, and then all is quiet except for the sounds of smacking and loud chewing.

My stomach growls as the cell door clinks closed next door, and I'm excited to finally be next. I must have slept through breakfast, but I'm more than ready to make up for it now. I take a few steps back toward my cot to give him room to open the door and pull the cart inside. Then, I watch as he slowly comes into view, and my heart claws its way up my throat.

"Uh . . ." Face to face with the most beautiful man I've ever seen, I forget my words.

I feel like I've been gut-punched, winded and staring wide-eyed as sex reincarnate stands there in front of me with a tray of food in his hand. A virtual wall of muscle, the guy practically emanates power. Standing a good six and a half or seven feet tall, anyone with sense would curl up in the corner and hide. But, all I can do is stand here and make little fish lips as I try to recover my speech.

He, on the other hand, seems quite in control, studying me shamelessly through the bars. And, though I'm practically naked, I feel it only fair that a little quid pro quo be established here, so I quickly get ahold of myself. Clacking my teeth together, I square my shoulders and begin a closer inspection of my own. I am, after all, not some bubble-headed dingbat easily seduced by her captors, no matter how hot they might be.

Having already taken note of his enormous girth, the next thing I notice is his long, blond hair. It hangs in thick, heavy sheets around his shoulders with tight, thin braids woven expertly throughout and laced at random intervals with little leather thongs. Loose-fitting pants that look like khakis, but not quite, stretch nicely across his abs and hang tenuously on his hips. The loose material only highlights the sheer, skin-tight shirt that hugs his perfect chest and clings nicely to the cords of ropey muscle that line his arms.

My mouth is full of cotton suddenly, and I have to lick my lips before I can speak again.

"Hi," is all I can manage to eke out.

He stares at me blankly for a moment, and just when I'm convinced that he either doesn't speak English or that he's all brawn and no brains, his lips curl into a delicious smile that makes my blood heat and my pussy clench. What is it about this guy?

"Hi," he finally replies, and his voice rolls over my skin like a warm breeze, causing a delightful shiver to run up my spine.

Geez! What the hell was that? Before I can figure it out, his smile broadens, revealing a very nice set of . . . fangs?

Seriously? I'm sure my eyes nearly pop out of my head, and I hear a mousy squeak puff from my lips.

"I will have to slide your food beneath the door. I don't have a key to your cell," he explains, now frowning as he shoves a tray beneath the bars.

"It's fine. Thank you," I tell him, shocked to my toes that I can actually understand him, at all. I take an unsure step toward the tray on the floor, watching him closely as I stoop to pick it up. Soft, golden eyes stare back at me, melting my insides and turning my muscles to mush.

"Tell me your name, little one."

"Aine. I'm Aine," I repeat, his deep, gravelly voice causing my brain to stutter for a moment. "Who are you?"

"Me? I'm just a slave," he tells me, cocking his head slightly as he eyes me curiously. "Like you."

A slave. Me? That's what Jill and Celia said, too, but . . . No, just no. I don't accept that. Maybe I'm nothing special or some important political figure, but that doesn't give some dickhead the right to kidnap me, slap a collar on me, and call me a slave. The notion really burns my ass.

My hands clench tightly around the tray until it feels like my knuckles might split, and I feel my face start to flame. I take a deep breath, reining in my temper before I say or do something I might regret. Then, I squint at him, trying to get a feel for where his allegiances lie. I need this guy's help. Slave or not, he's out there, and I'm locked in here. He has access to important things I need, things like keys.

"What's your name?"

"They call me Griz," he replies with a grin.

"Well, I guess I will, too, then." I smile back as sweetly as I can. "So, tell me Griz. How do we get out of here?"

# CHAPTER FOUR

Griz

My mate's name is Aine. I like it. Short and sweet, with a little bit of sass, just like her. It definitely suits her. She's been awake for less than an hour, and is already plotting her escape. I can see the wheels turning behind those gorgeous azure eyes. She's obviously smart, as well as beautiful. Feisty, too.

Maybe it was a frizzukish thing to do, but I told her she was a slave just to gauge her reaction. And, by the moons, she did not disappoint. Her demeanor became acute and deadly, and I caught a quick flash of anger before she'd been able to reel it back in. Yes, my delicate little flower has thorns.

Her entire body seemed to reject the very notion of enslavement, and for a moment, I thought she might actually break her food tray in half. It's clear she'll do whatever she must to get out of here. She will not let go of her freedom easily, not without a fight. That's what I need, her desperate for freedom. I will push her to her breaking point, hone her rage until she's ready to kill for it. There's a warrior inside her, I can tell.

Yes, this female is definitely my mate.

I smile at the sexy sparkle in her eye, and I can't stop sneaking peeks at her breasts, where her pretty pink nipples pebble and press against the thin fabric of her dress. She must realize the wayward direction of my thoughts because she crosses her arms over her chest and tips her exquisite little chin at me defiantly. I wonder if she knows just how hard that makes my cock?

"How do we get out of here?" she asks me, and my hearts swell with pride.

Already, she trusts me, her instincts pushing her to turn to her mate for protection. Her body knows exactly who I am, even if she does not.

My eyes comb the empty corridor, lingering briefly on the slave cells nearby.

"Not here," I tell her, my voice little more than a whisper. "It's not safe."

"Can you let me out?" she asks with hope in her tone, adjusting the volume of her voice to match mine.

I shake my head slowly. "No, meishkala. Only Beahl has the key. He won't trust anyone else with it."

She frowns at me, and a little vee forms between her eyebrows. I want to nuzzle it and lick it away.

"Why? And, why am I stuck in here all by myself?"

I stare at her curiously, and then it dawns on me. She really has no idea. "Because you are untouched, amavi."

"Untouched? What do you mean?" She quirks her mouth into a puzzled twist, her innocence cloaked around her like a palpable thing.

"Yes, Aine. You are pure and untouched," I tell her, but she still seems somewhat confused.

Perplexed, I take a deep breath and exhale slowly. Of all the times I've imagined being with my fated mate, and I admit, there have been many times, I never once envisioned myself having to explain the act of mating to her.

"You are a virgin, my little queen. No male has yet discovered your feminine secrets or dipped his cock into the sweet honey between your legs."

But I will. Soon. I smile, unable to contain my joy or my raging erection at the thought.

She gasps, her eyes growing wide as a lemurset's, and her

29

face turns a bright, vibrant red.

"But . . . What . . . How . . ." she stammers, obviously trying to recover her composure.

I bite back my grin, not wishing to embarrass my little mate any further.

"Just how the hell do you know *that*?" she suddenly demands with all the haughtiness of a queen and angry as a wet tigler.

"Ceazare performed an examination," I confess, rather uncomfortably.

She looks as though she might strangle me if she could reach me through the bars.

"While you were asleep," I add hastily, but it only makes things worse.

Her big, round eyes brim with tears, and her lower lip begins to tremble. Watching her, my hearts twist into a painful knot, and a lump settles in my throat. I should not have told her that.

"Did . . . Did he . . ." She sniffles. " . . . touch me?"

"No, amavi. I swear it. I would never have allowed it," I reassure her, stepping closer to the bars. I want her to know that I would kill for her, that I would gladly die for her honor, but I can't tell her that. Not yet.

She sniffs again and looks down at her feet. "I might be a virgin, but for your information, I am not *untouched*."

"It's okay, wee one. It's a good thing."

Her head snaps up, and she looks at me with fire in her eyes. "Yeah? Why's that? What's so good about it?"

*Because you saved yourself for me.*

"Because you were priceless before, and now, your value is doubled. You are more precious to Beahl than even his own dam. He has culled you from the others to keep his investment safe. Not even the guards can get to you now." I smirk.

Fear and anger flash across her face, and she balls her hands into little fists. "The guards? They would . . . you know . . . do that?"

Her eyes dart toward the cell next door, and then back to me.

It's obvious what she's thinking, and I bite my tongue, wishing that I could start over from the very beginning, and that she could keep her naivety for just a little while longer. But, no matter what I say now, she is bound to see things, hear things, that will leave a dark stain on her innocence forever. Her eyes hold me in place, silently demanding an answer, and I finally nod.

"Yes. They would."

Once again, fire blazes behind the calm azure sea of her eyes, and it makes me glad. Anger is good. It will get her through this. It will keep her alive and, eventually, show her the way to freedom.

Outside, I hear Lionese speaking with one of the guards. It wouldn't be good for him to see me talking to Aine. It wouldn't be good for him to see me in here at all since I actually stole the cart from one of the food bots to sneak back here to her.

"I have to go, but I'll come back. Know that you're safe, for now, mi amavi." At least, as safe as she can be for now. I turn and grip the food cart, preparing to push it back down the corridor.

"Griz, wait," she calls, and I turn to face her again.

I'm surprised to see that she's walked all the way up to the bars now and wrapped her little fingers tightly around them, her sweet face peeking out between the spindles.

I step even closer, close enough to touch her, but I don't. She's still too skiddish. I smile down at her, marveling that she barely reaches the top of my chest. My mate is small and petite. I will need to take extra care with her.

"What is it, little one?"

"There was a man," she says, biting her lip nervously.

"When they took me. I was with a man."

My hearts plummet into my stomach, and bile burns my throat. How could I have forgotten? Perhaps I had hoped that she wouldn't ask about him, wouldn't care enough to inquire. Perhaps, I feared my hearts would shatter into a million pieces if she told me that he was her mate. But he cannot be her amavi compar. Only I hold that precious honor. Jealousy wraps cold fingers around my intestines, squeezing and wringing my insides.

"Yes. The male is here. He is fine. He's being held in one of the private quarters away from the females," I tell her, dreading her reaction.

With good reason, I soon note as her eyes drift shut and her lips move in a silent prayer of thanks.

"Thank you," she says with a brilliant smile that nearly rips my hearts from my chest. Suddenly, she reaches through the bars and grasps my hand. "Thank you so much, Griz."

Startled, I flinch and nearly jerk away, but then, a heated rush moves through me at the feel of her little hand on mine. I stare fixedly into her eyes, working up the nerve to ask the thing I dread most knowing.

"This man, Aine. He is your . . . your . . ."

I can't do it. The word simply won't come out. The frizzuck'n thing is stuck in my throat, and I'm choking on it.

"Yes," she says, and I feel my soul begin to shrivel. "He's my pop."

"Your . . . *pop*?"

What the stars is a pop?

"Yes. My father. You know, my parent."

"The male is your sire?"

She giggles sweetly. "Yes, my *sire*, if you want to call it that. He's okay, though. Right?"

Sweet goddess! Thank the fates! Air swooshes back into my lungs, and I sag with relief as I raise her hand to my face, nuzzling it against my cheek and pressing my lips to her palm. Her sire! I'm so relieved, I have to laugh.

"You're sure he's all right?" she asks again, squinting at me suspiciously as I begin to sober.

"Yes, precious one. Your *pop* is fine. I will tell him that I've seen you, and that you are missing him."

The sparkle returns to her lovely eyes, and she graces me with another beautiful smile. "Yes, please do. Thank you, Griz."

"It's my pleasure, amavi." I give her hand one last nuzzle, determined to do whatever I can to win another one of those smiles later. "I'm going, but before I do, I need you to promise me something."

She looks at me curiously now. "Okay. What?"

"Promise me that you'll never, ever come this close to the bars again, especially when the guards are here."

She nods slightly, her face pinking, and she looks down at her feet again. "Of course. You're right. I know better."

"I care only for your safety, Aine," I tell her as I reach my hand through the bars and gently lift her face. I want her to see the truth in my eyes.

Her lips stretch into a shy smile.

"It might sound crazy, but I believe you," she says and then leans her face into my hand, nuzzling it sweetly.

Stars! She is so perfect.

"Now, I really do have to leave," I tell her. "Remember to stay well away from the bars, and don't anger the guards. Trust no one, and you'll be safe enough. I'll come back as soon as I can."

"All right."

I let my gaze linger on her for another brief moment, imprinting her succulent curves on my hearts and soul, so I can take the savory image with me.

*Soon, little amavi. Soon, you'll be mine.*

# CHAPTER FIVE

Aine

I can't help but wonder how many other girls are craning their necks and gawking at Griz's butt as he walks away. Still, I can't bring myself to feel bad about it. Things are just way too bad to deny myself a little pleasure. Besides, I'm not sure I could resist him even if I tried. There's something about the big protective alien that I just can't ignore, something besides muscles and good looks. I've never been so attracted to anyone, and he seems to genuinely care about me.

Turning around and leaning my back against the bars, I sigh and fan my face. I don't know if this giddy feeling is lust or love or something else entirely, but my pulse is still racing. I can't even think straight. All I can do is clench my thighs against the almost painful throbbing between my legs. I mean, I might be a virgin, but I'm no saint. And, it's not like my sexual condition is by choice. I swear Bruce has some kind of superhero cock-blocking powers that kick into overdrive whenever a guy gets too close to me.

The first time I tried going all the way, I was only seventeen. It's probably a good thing that Bruce was there to intervene, teenage hormones being what they are. I remember it like it was yesterday. Ray Person and I were nearly naked on his dad's pool table when Bruce called with a 9-1-1. My mum had collapsed in the middle of Target and had been rushed to the hospital in an ambulance. She never left the hospital again, and that was the last time I recall feeling anything even remotely close to normal.

It was almost two years before I worked up enough courage to try the sex thing again. Alone at home with Philip Comer, we were making out on the couch in our underwear when Bruce burst through the front door singing Bonnie Leezie Lindsay with a fifth of whiskey in one hand and a nine iron in the other. I don't think it was intentional. I found out later that he'd been playing golf with his friend, Ernie, at the country club. Anyway, I don't know who was most shocked — me, Philip, or Bruce. He ended up chasing Philip out of the house with the nine-iron, and the poor boy had to run all the way home in his skivvies. The ordeal left me permanently scarred.

Still, I wasn't ready to totally give up. I just haven't had much time for dating over the past twelve months. Pop lost his job as an electrician shortly after Lachlin disappeared, and times have since been tough. Even so, I'd considered seducing a co-worker or just going to the club one night and picking up a one-night stand, more to get rid of the virgin label than because I was horny. That just didn't seem like a good-enough reason to risk my reputation or a pregnancy or some awful sexually transmitted disease. So, here I am, a twenty-year-old virgin, almost as rare as a unicorn these days.

"Aine! What did he say to you? Could you understand him?" Jill interrupts my musings as soon as the heavy metal door at the end of the hall clangs shut. "Aine?"

"What?" I ask stupidly, even though I heard every word she said. I'm just not sure what to tell her, especially in light of the "trust no one" comment Griz made.

"Were you guys talking? What'd he say?" she asks excitedly, her questions tumbling over each other.

"Um . . . Yeah. I mean, he was speaking to me, but I don't know exactly what he was saying," I reply, immediately feeling guilty for lying to the only other person who's been nice to me. Maybe Celia was right. Maybe it is every woman for herself in here.

"That sure was a lot of talking for you guys not to understand each other," Celia accuses.

"He was throwing a lot of hand gestures."

"I bet. I can just imagine the kinds of hand gestures he was throwing," Celia snorts.

Times like these, my pop always quotes Mark Twain. Well, tries to quote him, rather, but he rarely ever gets it quite right. "Never argue with an idiot. They will drag you down to their level and beat you with experience." Something tells me that Celia is very experienced.

"I'm going to eat now. I'm starving," I inform them, heading for my little cot and taking my tray of lukewarm food with me.

They continue chattering and speculating, but I do my best to ignore them. Now that I know Bruce is okay, the brick that had been lodged in my stomach feels much lighter. So, rather than dwell on the hundred gazillion questions I have, I opt to focus on my food instead.

Using a utensil that looks more like a chopstick than a fork, I poke at a thick slab of meat that reminds me of steak. Except that it's blue. Next to it, there's a blob of something that's an orangish color with the consistency of potatoes, and finally, what I assume is the vegetable portion of the meal—a purple leafy plant smothered in a grey sauce that smells great, but looks like something a cat spit up. I take a deep breath and dig in. I will not be defeated by feline vomit.

Twenty minutes later, feeling full and surprisingly satisfied, I nudge the tray back under the cell bars with my toe. I have no idea what I just ate, but it was actually better than a lot of meals I've had back home, especially when Bruce does the cooking. I barely make it back to my cot when the sound of clanking keys has me turning around and flitting back to the bars again.

Is Griz back so soon? Maybe he has a message from Bruce? My pulse quickens with excitement, my breath heavy with expectation, as I wait on tiptoes to see Griz's spectacular form lumbering toward me any moment.

But it's not Griz.

"We jussst got a new batch in last night," a high-pitched, nasally voice all but hisses.

So, it's not just Griz that I can understand. I can understand these guys, too.

"Really? What kind?" a throaty, rumbly voice asks.

"Mostly Balquers and Lypherians, but there's a few Earthersss, too. All good quality."

"You got Earthers here?"

"Yesss. Back there," the first guy hisses, and I hear them coming toward our cells.

Slinking back toward my cot, I try to make myself disappear. I mean, it doesn't take a rocket scientist to figure out these guys are bad news, and Griz and Jill have already warned me. I hear them stop next door, and though I feel bad for Jill and Celia, I'm glad they're not coming in here. I take the opportunity to curl up in a little ball on my cot and toss the thin, smelly blanket over my head.

As I hunker beneath the blanket quivering, a small pang of guilt hits me. I should be trying to help the other girls, not hide here like a coward. Then again, there's nothing I can do for them. I'm locked behind thick, iron bars, and even if I wasn't, if they're anywhere near as big as Griz, there's no way I could take them. I almost wish I knew what they looked like, so I'd know if I stood a fighting chance.

Clanking keys on the cell door and a chorus of gasps and screams tells me all I really need to know. Big, scary aliens. Got it. I don't need to know any more than that.

"The Earthersss are in here," the first guy says.

"Nice. I like the look of that Lypherian there, too. But, look how smooth that one's skin is."

I can tell they're walking around by the way their voices fade and then get louder.

"Quiet!" the nasally guy screams, and I hear a loud slap followed by a whimper, and then deafening silence.

"Never too soon to start training them right, eh?" The guy with the deep, throaty voice chuckles.

There's a long hiss in response, which I assume is the first guy laughing.

"Ssso, which will it be?"

"I don't know. I can't decide between these two and that Lypherian over there," he says, and then there's a pause as he seems to consider. "I thought you said there were three Earthers?"

No, no, no. Don't come back here.

"Yesss. There were three. The other must be in one of those cellsss."

"I think I like this one."

I hear footsteps, and then the sound of Jill's panicked voice.

"No! No. Please don't!" she begs, and the hair on my arms stand on end.

"I said quiet!"

The sound of another slap ends with her sobbing. Tears burn the backs of my eyelids, and a multitude of emotions assail me. Torn between crippling fear, murderous anger, and a burning hatred that nearly swallows me up, my body trembles like a dried-up leaf.

"I want to see its breasties."

The sound of fabric ripping has me on the edge of my cot, and then, Jill's cries turn into screams.

Another slap, and the rest of the women join her so that soon, everyone is screaming. Fear like I've never known turns my blood to ice, and I'd crawl beneath my cot if it was possible.

"Mm. Those are nice, but it only has two. I get twice that, plus six cock holes for half the price with the Lypherian."

"That's true, but I hear the Earthers' holes are like heaven. They say once you stick your cock in one, it could be days before you pull it back out again."

"Really? Still, it's a lot of quarvos to spend for only two breasties. Let me see its holes first."

Jill screams again, and I cover my ears with my hands, squeezing my eyes shut as tight as I can.

"Leave her alone!" Celia's voice rings out, and I hear yet another slap.

But there's no crying that follows this time.

"What's it doing?"

"I think it likesss you," the snaky voice says and then hisses its laughter.

"Yeah, that's right. Wouldn't you rather have someone a little more experienced?" Celia asks in a deep, throaty voice. "Take me, you limp-peckered frog-faced bastard, and leave her alone."

Her voice is now a seductive purr, and I can't believe what I'm hearing. Celia is sacrificing herself for Jill? Maybe she's not the mean, selfish bitch I thought she was? Maybe there's hope for us, after all?

# CHAPTER SIX

Griz

Stepping inside the extra quarters where Aine's sire is being held is like stepping into a different dimension. The room is generally used to house Beahl's guests, so while it's not enormous, it's still clean and hospitable, opulent compared to the slave cells. I won't dare tell him that, though, even after I find him. Right now, I don't see him anywhere.

Holding a tray of food in my hand, I shove the door closed with my foot while I scan the room. I know I left him here last night.

Suddenly, there's a loud crash, then a sharp pain begins to bloom at the back of my head. A shower of glass splinters follows, raining down on my shoulders and exploding across the room. Was that Beahl's favorite teapot?

"Whoa! Calm down." I whirl around, balancing a tray of food in one hand, trying to subdue the crazy male who's trying to kill me with the other. Surprisingly, he's a lot stronger than he looks. Even so, I could easily crush him like a flicker-bug, but I won't hurt my mate's sire.

"I'll kill you, you boaby headed bawbag," he yells, continuing on with a string of non-sensical words that I can only assume are threats of some kind.

My translator keeps bleeping and erring out over and over, but I think I get the gist. Still, unless he has a molecular recomp disintegration device stuffed in his pants, I'm not too worried.

"Stop! I have a message from Aine," I shout.

The male immediately stills, his mouth drawing into a grim line and his eyes narrowing into little slits. I can see the same intelligent glint in them that I saw in my mate's, and they're the exact same azure color. The resemblance is clear now. He still hasn't replied to my claim, though, and I know he's trying to decide if it's a trick or a trap.

"She's here, and she wanted me to tell her pop that she's fine," I add, hoping to gain some measure of his trust.

"Aine," he groans. "Where is she? What have you done to her?"

"She's being held on the other side of the ship, and I would never do anything to harm her," I explain as I study his tray of food, now covered in little shards of glass. He certainly can't eat it like this. "I'll have to bring you something else to eat later."

"Feck the food, lad. Bring me daughter to me. Now!"

"Would that I could," I tell him as I set the tray back down, contemplating his strange accent. Why does he speak so differently than Aine? "Unfortunately, that's not within my power. I'm afraid I'm as much a prisoner here as you are."

"You're a prisoner?"

Nodding, I set the tray down on a small table in the living space. "This ship is the property of Beahl Vellander DeCombre, supreme leader of the Lizentine Empire," I tell him. "And, so are we, I'm afraid."

Bruce gives me an indignant look. "That's where you're wrong, lad. I am Bruce Liam MacTavish, supreme leader of the MacTavish Empire of Earth, and I am no man's property."

I nearly chortle at his pompous assertion, but manage to control myself. Somehow, I don't think this male will take too kindly to being laughed at. It's easy to see where Aine gets her fire, though. I wave toward one of the small chairs in the corner.

41

"May we sit for a moment? I don't have much time, but we need to talk. If that's okay with you?" I raise my brow, waiting for any objections.

He gives a sharp nod then pulls out a chair to sit down.

"Speak fast and keep to the point. I can't abide no blethering bampot today," he says, though I have no idea what a blethering bampot is or why my language download is erring out so much. "I've got a headache."

"I understand. I'll be brief. First of all, my name is Griz."

"I done told you my name is Bruce."

"You prefer Bruce to 'Pop?'"

"From you? Yes. Definitely."

I nod in deference. Soon, it will be Honored Sire of my Beloved Mate, but Bruce will do for now. "Fine, Bruce. You do realize that you've been captured by a race of Lizentine warriors and taken off-planet. Yes?"

He glances toward the window that gives a perfect view of deep space and then cuts his eyes back to me. "What kind of wallaper do I look like to you? Of course I know that."

"Of course you do," I reply, nodding complacently and biting back a grin. In many ways, this human is like a big youngling. "That said, you should also know that I'm planning to escape, and I want to take you and Aine with me. But, I need your help."

It's his turn to cock a brow at me now. "Seems to me you're pretty free to come and go as you please already. I can barely help myself. I can't even leave this room."

"Ah. It might appear that way, but I'm not so free as you might think. Neither are you, and nor is Aine, for that matter. Don't let the lack of chains fool you. We each have implants that will, for all intents and purposes, blow up if we wander more than eight-hundred meters from the detonator."

"Implants, you say?"

I lean over to touch the spot on his head where the implant

is embedded, and he flinches.

"I thought I just bumped it. I woke up this morning with a hellacious headache, and bruises all over me."

Probably best not to tell him that it's from Lionese dragging him up the steps to the ship last night. He already looks half-cocked and ready to go off, and he's pointed right at me.

"So, you can see," I go on. "While I'm not locked in a cell all day, my movements are still strictly limited."

"So, what do you want me to do? I'm not saying that I'll do it, mind you. I'll get me and Aine out of here one way or another, anyway. If I have to fight this guy . . . Bill or Bell . . . what's his name?"

"Beahl."

"Whatever. If I have to fight him, that's fine with me. I'll kick the shite out of him, cut this implant thing out of my head, and waltz right out of here. And, I'll be taking my daughter with me," he adds, squinting his accusing eyes at me.

I smile with approval. This male is a warrior, too. Though, I shouldn't be surprised. Aine had to have gotten it from somewhere. Still, does he not understand that if it was just a matter of fighting someone, I would have been free long ago?

"Beahl is never without his guards. You wouldn't be able to get him alone long enough to fight him, and even then, I'm not sure you could overpower him. Challenging would do you no good, either. He has no honor. Even if you were able to fight him and, by some miracle, beat him, he'd just activate the implant from the remote as soon as he was able."

"Then, I'll kill him. Problem solved."

"The implant is set to explode automatically if Beahl's life functions cease or in the event it's removed prior to deactivation. So, you see, he doesn't need chains to control us, and it's in our best interest to make sure he stays alive."

"So, what's your plan, then? And, what does it have to do

with me and my Aine?"

"We're on our way to Janyx," I tell him, waiting for the weight of my words to sink in.

"Okay." He stares blankly back at me. "What's Janyx?"

Shaking my head, I growl at myself. Of course he would not have heard of Janyx before. Earth is part of Sector Six, not yet developed enough for space exploration, and forbidden to space travelers. Not that it stops people like Beahl from going there.

"The primary auction house in Sector Three is located on Janyx. It's where everyone in the galaxy goes to purchase slaves — pleasure houses, noblemen, royalty, politicians. Basically, anyone with enough coin in his pockets goes to Janyx to purchase their slaves."

"Pleasure houses?" His forehead creases, and he scowls at me.

"Yes. Beahl intends to sell Aine as a pleasure giver at auction."

"Over my dead body," he roars, standing up so fast, his chair nearly tips over.

"That may very well be the case," I calmly inform him. "Unless we can stop him. Beahl plans to sell you, too, as a house slave, but he'll have to train you first if he wants top quarvos at auction. And, knowing Beahl, he always wants top quarvos. This is where your help will be needed."

"Train, my arse. Where is this alien diddy? I'm going to kill him, implant be damned."

"And, Aine, too? Because that's what would happen."

"Shite!" He paces back and forth. "We might have a problem there. You see, I'm not really trainable, and I'm definitely not the slave type."

"Bruce, if you don't cooperate, Beahl will kill you. It's as simple as that. I'm working on a plan, but I need your help. I can't get into Beahl's quarters, and I'm never left alone on the bridge. I'll never have the access that you will. I only ask that you go along with the plan until we can escape."

If I have to beg, I will. I cannot let my mate lose her sire, and it's my fault he's here in the first place. She might never forgive me if something happens to him.

"Why should I trust you?" he asks boldly.

I tap my finger on the chair as I think. It's a fair question.

"What choice do you really have?" I hate having to point this out to him, but I have no choice. If we're to succeed, I must have his help.

He considers my words. He knows that I'm right, but his pride won't let him admit it. "What if he hurts Aine?"

*Then, I will kill him myself.*

"He will shove you through the airlock into space without a second thought, and then, who would be left to watch over your Aine?" I would, of course, but no need to tell him that. "I will do my best to protect her in the meantime."

He leans against the chair and puffs out his chest. "I am Bruce Liam MacTavish, descended from Robert the Bruce, and my daughter's line can be traced all the way back to the great William Wallace. She is Scottish royalty, a princess of the Isles. Anyone who lays a finger on her dies."

Royalty? A princess? Aine is a princess? That makes total sense. Her beauty, her courage, the regal way she holds her chin. I make a note of the names Bruce gave me so I can look them up on the ship's computer. That knowledge might be useful later. Then, I frown. Aine is royalty. I am only a cousin to the king. Is that royal enough to mate her? Will her sire accept my claim?

Bruce's burly voice interrupts my thoughts.

"I will fight, lad. But, I'm not stupid. I know that when the going gets tough, no man is an island. We'll try it your way first."

"Thank you," I tell him with a slight jerk of my chin, though his words seem to make no sense. "Why is it that you speak so differently from Aine?"

"You noticed that, eh?" He smiles. "I was born in the old country. Moved to the States when I was still a young man and took my wife and new son with me. We had Aine soon after we got there. It's all she's ever known. She's never even stepped foot on our native soil."

"You were exiled?"

"Aye. I guess you could say that."

"And, the language is so different between your old home and your new home."

"Aye. Everything is different. Or, was different, I guess."

A horrible thought occurs to me, and my hearts nearly wilt in my chest. "We've left Aine's dam on Earth unprotected?"

"You mean her mum? Aine's mum died five years ago."

"So, it's just you, your son and Aine?"

"It's just me and Aine now. Her brother, Lachlan, up and disappeared last year. I'm afraid I've been a piss-poor excuse of a father ever since. Well, longer than that, I suppose. Since her blessed mum passed. But, I intend to make up for that," he says, determination shining in his steely blue eyes.

My poor mate. She's known so much loss in her short span. I get up to leave, bowing respectfully to my mate's father. "I have to go, but I'll come back later, and we'll discuss the details of our plan. And, Bruce . . . ."

He glares at me as if to let me know I'm working his patience. The corner of my lips twitch as I once again try not to smile.

"For now, it might not be wise to let Beahl know that Aine is your daughter. He would certainly leverage the information against you."

"You sound like you know that from experience."

He's perceptive, too. "I do. He's holding my dam on Janyx."

"The bastard's got your mum?"

"He is ruthless," I warn.

I leave before he can ask me anything else about it. I'm not really in a good place to think about what my dam is going through right now. Shoving the stolen food cart into one of the small maintenance closets that line the corridors, I hurry back toward my room. I barely make it around the next corner before Beahl calls out to me.

"Griz!"

Cringing, I turn to face him. "Yes?"

"Yes, *master*. You are a terrible slave, Griz." He shakes his head as if exasperated by my performance. His guard reaches a hand toward the welter whip at his waist, anticipating an order that doesn't come.

"Yes," I say, just to irritate him. "I'll try to do better."

"I doubt that. Anyway, I was thinking. Since it will take us a couple of cycles to reach Janyx, and we'll be flying through several more quadrants that are ripe for picking, maybe we'll squeeze in one more raid before we get there. I think we have room, and even if we don't, they can just double up."

"They're already sleeping on top of each other," I tell him, hoping to change his mind.

"Well, then. It's good practice for them," he says with a cruel smile. "They need to get used to having someone on top of them. Figure it out, but I want more females. Study the map, and outline for me a plan with the least risk and the highest reward. This haul should be enough that I won't have to leave the palace again for a very long time. Maybe ever."

"Yes," I reply, envisioning all the various ways I could kill the evil bastard.

More victims. Still, this could prove to be our best way out. Escape would certainly be easier than if we waited to reach Janyx.

*But, what about my dam?*

# CHAPTER SEVEN

Aine

The door at the end of the hall suddenly crashes open, and a new voice bellows down the corridor.

"What the hell's going on in here?"

I hear the men in the cell next door tripping over themselves to clamber out. "Lionessse. I was just showing Grimmut here the stock."

"Hm. Showing him the stock? I can just imagine." The new guy doesn't sound all that convinced. "The auction doesn't begin until we reach Janyx, Shan."

"Of course, sir. Grimmut just wanted to pick one out to bid on."

"Look what you did to their faces, you idiot!" I hear another slap, but this time, it sounds as though the guard is the recipient, not Jill or Celia. "Do not lay a finger on these Earthers again. If you've permanently marked them—"

"I barely touched them," the guard lies. "Besides, they'll have plenty of time to heal before we get there."

"You know nothing of Earthers, fool. They're more fragile than the others, and we have no idea how long their healing process is. Just look at that one's eye! Let me see the other female. If you've touched her, Shan, so help me, Beahl will gut you, after I've skinned you."

"It must be in one of the other cells. I haven't even seen it yet."

Still hiding under my blanket, I try not to vomit as I hear

footsteps shuffling toward me.

"She's in here. Beahl put her in this one last night," the one called Lionese says.

I'm still hiding, quivering beneath my blanket, but I can feel their eyes burning holes in me.

"You! Earther! Stand up and let me see you," Lionese shouts.

I'm not sure what to do. Maybe he'll think I don't understand him. Please, lord, let him give up and go away.

"It doesn't understand you," one of them croaks.

"Yes, she does. Ceazare gave her a language download last night. She knows exactly what I'm saying," he tells them. Then, he addresses me again. "Earther, get up. I won't tell you again."

Fuck. What should I do? I thought Griz said they couldn't get to me? Slowly, I push my head out of the covers, but freeze when I get my first good look at them.

Two of them resemble lizards, except they're standing upright and they're every bit as tall as Griz. Not to mention, they have long, thick tails! Their eerie eyes are an iridescent yellow with diamond-shaped pupils and what looks like a second clear lid that skates over their eyeballs when they blink. They have enormous oblong faces like a lizard with little slits for nostrils, and a long, ribboned tongue that undulates like a snake's when they speak. Their teeth are sharp and pointy, with four larger fangs on top and on the bottom. They're both covered in swampy-colored scales, their throats a luminous green.

One of them has already started fumbling with his keys, trying to unlock my cell.

"Don't waste your time," Lionese tells him.

"It won't open," the guard says, confused.

"I told you not to waste your time. Beahl made me put a different lock on her door."

"Why would he do that?"

He gives the guard a knowing look, clearly disgusted. "To protect her from the likes of you, froekhead. This one is off-limits. Off-limits to you, to him, and to all the other stiff-dicks out there. She's untouched, and she's worth billions."

"She's untouched?"

The other alien, silent to this point, leaps excitedly onto the bars, and I nearly gag when I see him.

He reminds me of a toad, and from the way he's panting and the tent he's pitching in his pants, a horny one, at that. This guy has slits for nostrils, too, but the similarity ends there. His dark green, bumpy skin looks wet and slimy, and he only has three fingers on each hand, every one knobby and webbed. His big, round eyes bulge excitedly as he stares at me, rubbing himself against the bars.

"Yes, and she will remain that way until after auction," Lionese says as he leers at the toad man. "Don't even think about it, Balda. You don't have enough credits to even sniff her pussy, and you wouldn't live long enough afterward to enjoy the memory. Now, stand up, female."

Nuh-uh. Not happening. I couldn't stand up right now if I wanted to. My legs feel like spaghetti.

"You should know, Earther, that just because I can't open the door right now, there are still a great many ways I can hurt you. So, don't let the locked door fool you. Now, stand up before I get my welter whip."

Reluctantly, I push off the covers and stand up, letting all three of them ogle me like a prize calf at the county fair.

"Come here, Earther," Lionese says.

Fuck you. I shake my head.

"Come here. Now," he yells.

I flinch, but don't do it. Hell, a raging fire in my cell couldn't make me go any closer to him. Slowly, he moves his hand toward a fuzzy-like cotton coil attached to his hip. I swallow hard and shake my head again. I promised Griz I wouldn't, and somehow, I think my fate would be worse if I were to do as he says.

Just as he shakes out the fuzzy-looking piece of rope, the big door at the end of the hall opens once again.

"Lionese!" someone shouts. "You're needed in engineering."

"I'll be right there," he snarls in reply.

The big, ugly lizard man narrows his eyes at me.

"You're lucky this time," he spits, and then turns to his companions. "You two, get the haelic out of here, and don't let me catch you back here again."

Grumbling, the two guards turn around and head back down the hall while Lionese turns to me one more time and gives me a barbarous smile.

"And, you, female, will learn to obey me," he says, and then lashes out at me with his fluffy whip.

The long, soft strip of wooly cotton lands against my leg, and at first, it almost tickles. I'm on the verge of laughing when suddenly my thigh feels like it's catching on fire. A hot, burning streak of pain shoots up and down my leg and spreads throughout my entire body. Pain like I've never felt before, couldn't even comprehend before. I fall to the floor, gasping for breath and writhing in agony.

Holy fuck nuggets! What the hell was that?

"Next time, I'll stripe you all over," he threatens, though I can't imagine how I could hurt any worse without dying. With one last hateful glare, he turns on his heel and walks away. Thank God.

Almost afraid to look at my leg, I force my eyes to focus on the spot that hurts the worst. I half expect it to be hanging by a few threads where the rope landed, but I'm relieved to see there's only a slight red welt where he struck me on my thigh. Even so, holy cow. I'm still shaking from the mind-numbing aftershocks, and I don't think it's going to subside anytime soon. Note to self—avoid the soft, wooly rope thingies at all costs!

Dragging my throbbing leg behind me, I hobble over to the bars, clutching at them to pull myself upright. I might have a little ache in my leg, but poor Jill's injuries run much deeper than mine.

"Jill?" I call out, not surprised when she doesn't answer. "Celia, how is she? How's Jill?"

"What do you care?" Celia answers.

"I . . . Why . . ." Her response really chaps my ass. Still hurting, now, I'm so angry I can hardly speak. "That's just shitty. Of course I care! Why wouldn't I care? She's the only person who's been nice to me since I got here."

*Besides Griz.*

"Jill's nice to everyone," she says after a pause.

"Not quite everyone," Jill replies. "I'd kill that slimy lizard asshole if I could. Him and his bug-eyed boyfriend."

"Maybe we'll get the chance," I tell her. "I don't know about you, but I'm not going to just sit around waiting to be sold like chattel to the highest bidder. I'm getting out of here."

"We all want out of here," Celia snips. "Easier said than done when we're locked up in here without even a bobby pin between us to use as a weapon."

"Not to mention there's an army of froggy lizard men out there, each one the size of a Sherman tank. Besides, where would we even go if we did somehow miraculously manage to get free? You know how to fly a spaceship?" Jill adds resignedly.

"We've got to get out here!" a girl shouts from their cell. It's a new, unfamiliar voice, and it catches me by surprise. "Don't you idiots know what they're going to do to us?"

"Who's that?" I shout back excitedly.

"I don't know. Some crazy crab chick over here. She's red and has pinchers the size of Jill's ass."

"Gee, thanks," Jill snipes.

"She keeps chanting weird stuff like 'kumu lotta pucosh' or something. We try to just ignore her," Celia says.

*Kumu lotta pucosh.* Let us die with honor. Somehow, I know what that means. I don't know how I know, but I do. What the hell?

"They're going to sell us to animals!" the girl shrieks. "They'll beat us, fuck us, and torture us, if they don't rut us to death first!"

"Can you not understand what she's saying?" I ask, desperate for answers.

"Of course not. Are you saying that you can? It's just a bunch of gibberish."

I rest back against the bars, shaking my head at the floor. How can I understand her, and no one else can? It makes no sense.

"I need to think," I say to no one in particular. Hauling my aching leg back over to my cot, I lie down on my smelly blanket and let my eyes drift shut. There has to be a way out of this.

I need to figure out this weird communication situation first. It seems I can understand Jill and Celia, and they can understand me. But, they can't understand anyone else, and no one else can understand them. I, on the other hand, can understand everyone, but not everyone can understand me.

This is just too crazy to contemplate without coffee. How can I plan a coup this way? Bruce's words about revolutions float through my mind, and I smile ruefully. Did William Wallace have these kinds of issues? My head is hammering from the lack of caffeine, the pain of the welter whip, and trying to figure out the crazy communication puzzle. Before long, my thoughts begin to drift.

*Clink. Clang. Ping. Whir. Clink. Clang. Ping. Whir.*
What the hell is that? My eyelids flutter open, and I sit up,

resting back my elbows as I blink the sleep from my eyes. *Still here, dammit.* I had hoped it was all a bad dream.

Once I can see straight, I look around curiously, trying to find the source of the strange noises that woke me up. When I do find it, I have to wonder if I'm not still dreaming, after all.

A tall, blue female—I say *female* because I'm not really sure that I can call her a girl or a woman—in a dress similar to mine, but red in color, stands outside my cell. She picks up a tray from a dingy grey cart, the same kind of cart that Griz served me from earlier, and holds it out toward my cell. I know she's trying to show me the food, but I can't tear my eyes away from her.

Her movements are choppy and jerkish, and her eyes roll around in their luminous sockets like heavy, black marbles. And, if that alone isn't enough to freak me out, then, the strange noises coming out from under her dress certainly are. *Clink. Clang. Ping. Whir.*

"Good evening, prisoner eight four six nine two. On tonight's menu, we have baked lascava with wild frippo sauce, quadraloons, and tarsel snaps," she says, her voice cold and robotic. "Enjoy your meal, eight four six nine two."

I'm still gawping from my cot when she shoves the tray under the bars and swivels back around to her cart, wheeling it leisurely down the hallway. I drop my eyes to the tray of food, and my stomach growls on queue. Once again, everything smells wonderful, but it looks like a rainbow has curled up and died on my plate.

I toss the covers aside and stand up slowly to test my leg. Thankfully, it feels fine now, no more pain, and it's not even red anymore. Easing toward the tray, I listen carefully, hoping to figure out the other loud, annoying sound I keep hearing. Quickly, I realize that fifty people smacking at the same time in the same close quarters is not conducive to one's appetite.

A few minutes later, I'm taking my last bite of lascava with wild frippo sauce, which tastes just like chicken-fried steak, and I'm stuffed. I stand up and stretch as I glance around, wondering again if there are any hidden cameras or microphones in my cell. I still don't find any, which is a relief because I really need to pee. Not that a camera would have stopped me, but I'm driven by a need to know. I've already had to use the toilet in the corner a couple of times, and I still don't feel any better about it. I can't even imagine what they're going through next door.

Two minutes and two pieces of oval, sponge-like toilet tissue later, I'm back on my cot staring at the ceiling again. It's clear that if the guards don't kill me, the boredom of this place surely will. I need a plan. I can't count on this cell to keep me safe forever. Lionese made it clear that he can hurt me any time he wants, and one wrong move outside this cell, and I'll have every hard dick on the ship flying at me. I have to get out of here.

Not for the first time, I wish I had a cup of coffee. A Marlboro would be nice, too. I don't really smoke, but I like the feel of a good cigarette between my lips when I'm contemplating a problem. Sometimes, I don't even light them. I just hold them there and pretend to smoke.

Think, think, think .... How can we do this? There are enough of us to fight back if we can just coordinate an attack. Though, how can I coordinate anything when I can't even communicate with the other prisoners? When I can't see past my own cell? The thought of getting out of our cells just to get caught and raped, maybe even killed, on the other side of the door is enough of a deterrent to make me second-guess everything. Maybe we'd at least all survive if we stay here and do nothing. But, would we even want to by the time they're through with us?

Tears pool in my eyes, and I swipe them away angrily. Crying's not going to get me anywhere. If there was ever a time to be strong, it's now, and if I can get through my mum's death and my brother's disappearance without shedding a tear, I can damn sure get through this.

*You were born to lead revolutions, lass.*

"We're about to see, Bruce."

# CHAPTER EIGHT

Griz

"This is it? This is your recommendation?" Beahl waves the parchment at me as if my plan is ridiculous.

"Yes," I reply drolly. If he wants enthusiasm, he should have sent for me after lunch, and not in the wee hours of the morning. I haven't even had any kova yet.

"Yes, *master*," he reminds me once again with irritation. Doesn't sound like he's had his kova yet, either. "Perhaps a few days in isolation will help you remember that? Maybe a few lashes with Lionese's welter whip? Would that help?"

I can't go in isolation, not right now. I can't leave Aine there by herself, and I need to work on my plan with Bruce. We don't have much time.

"No, *master*. I won't forget again," I grit out around the burning bile in my throat.

"We'll see," he replies skeptically, his eyes hard and suspicious as they regard me. "Now, tell me why you're recommending Kerberos for the raid."

Of all the planets between here and Janyx, Kerberos gives us our best chance at escape. Mostly wooded and undeveloped, its citizens are primarily simple farmers and unlikely to be aligned with any criminal elements. Export ships come and go frequently, and I'm sure we can hop a ride on one fairly easily.

I do my best to look indifferent about the whole thing. If he thinks I want to go to Kerberos, he'll disregard it right out of the gate, no matter how good the plan is.

"It doesn't really matter to me. You asked me to work up a recommendation. There it is. Kerberos poses the least amount of security risk and has the largest variety of females. As you know, it's full of pacifists and draft dodgers from all across the universe, those who've fled there for asylum with their families. The planet is diverse and practically unprotected."

Beahl nods, his eyes still squinty and sharp. I can tell he's thinking about his bottom line and how easy these pickings would be. Then, his lips curve into a serpentine smile, and I can breathe again. I've got him.

"I think you're onto something here, Griz. I like your strategy. See now why I didn't wipe your memories when the Goridians first gave you to me? There's a lot of good skill and training locked in there, and it would be a shame to lose all that." He jabs at his head for emphasis. "Those Tarileans know how to train their warriors. All you needed was a little bit of motivation."

It takes everything in me to keep from curling my hands into fists and driving them through his scaly, reptilian face.

"Is my dam okay?"

"Of course, of course. She's fine. Her new master is treating her very well, I hear. Let's you and I work together to make sure it stays that way."

His threat is not so much veiled as obvious. Yes, I will kill him very slowly, very soon. Even if it means my own death to get the job done. Dying would surely be worth it so long as I could take him with me.

"Like this," he says, tapping the parchment with his long, knobby finger. "This is good work, Griz. Now, how soon before we get to Kerberos?"

"Three spans." Not much time to prepare, but it's the best chance we've got.

"Good. Good. Work with Lionese to make sure everything is in order, and we'll plan on Kerberos in three spans."

He turns his attention back to his desk and begins shuffling through various parchments and flip tablets. I take that as a dismissal and turn to leave.

"Stop! I didn't tell you that you could go," he says in his nasally, high-pitched voice that makes my fingers twitch to rip out his hearts.

I turn around and level him with hate-filled eyes that promise death. But, the froeckhead is too stupid to be scared. He should be, though.

"Right now, I need you to bring the human male to my chambers. You were right. He's way too small to make a good field hand. Huberus over there is going to start training him as a house slave. We'll see how he does."

"Right away . . . master," I reply, secretly thrilled that my plans are falling into place. This just might work, after all.

"Huberus!"

Beahl's favorite house bot steps forward to stand beside me.

"Yes, master," he says, gesticulating properly with a bow.

"Go to my chambers and prepare to receive a new trainee, the male that Griz is bringing to you. Start him off with the basics, and teach him as much as you can before we get to Janyx. You have about two cycles to get him to pass as a halfway decent house servant."

"Yes, master," Huberus says with another bow, this one much deeper. Then, he turns and gives me an impressive glare, which is quite a feat for an AI droid.

"Good. Now, get out. I'm quite busy," he says as he waves his hands impatiently at us.

I follow Huberus out of the office, feeling light and optimistic now that I finally have a plan. "I'll meet you shortly. I have to go get the human."

"I'll leave the door open to allow you entry," he says almost proudly, knowing that he is the only other person or bot on the ship able to enter Beahl's quarters.

It doesn't take long to reach Bruce's door, and I rap on it lightly. Understandably, there's no answer. It's still early, so I doubt he's even up yet. I'm about to knock again when the door swings wide open, and Bruce stands in the doorway. Scowling. Naked.

"Uh . . . ." The shock of my soon-to-be sire-in-law fresh from slumber with his free-swinging cock prostrating upright in the doorway has me a bit off-kilter.

"Well? You've dragged me out of my bed. So, speak, ye dunderheid."

"Apologies, sire — I mean, Bruce." He has me so flustered, I can barely remember my own name, much less his. What's wrong with me? I'm a well-trained, highly skilled and blooded warrior. It should take more than a floppy cock to get me rattled. "Beahl wishes for you to begin your training."

"Right now?"

I watch him, fascinated, as one hand moves to scratch his head and the other to scratch his ass simultaneously. Repulsive, but I can't help but admire his dexterity. And, this male is royalty on Earth?

"Yes," I reply, biting my lip to keep from laughing. His hair is now sticking out all over the place, and he reminds me of a Mongerian yakos.

"Man can't even get a decent night's sleep around here," he grouses as he stands aside and motions for me to come in. I enter against my better judgment.

"Beahl is an early riser, as you can see."

"Well, the early bird flocks together, I suppose. Or, something like that. Have a seat while I find my pants." He waves his hand toward the guest chairs.

I do my best to avert my eyes, but the crazy male is all over the place. Every time I turn my head, he's there. Either he's displaying his neon white ass as he hops around trying to get his feet into his pant legs or scouring the floor for socks or dancing around to put on his shoes. At least, he's covered now.

"There. I guess I'm ready." He tugs on the hem of his shirt and then scrubs a large, calloused hand down his face.

"Good. But, you might want to . . . um . . . ," I gesture toward my hair, hoping he'll take the hint.

He narrows his eyes, giving me a dangerous look. "What? Comb your hair?"

I succumb to a fit of coughing.

"Fates, no! Comb your own hair," I choke out.

"Oh. That's probably not a bad idea," he mumbles more to himself than to me, and then disappears into the refresher.

I shake my head, wondering if he's like this all the time. If so, his mate certainly had her hands full.

"Say, you wouldn't happen to have a drop of whisky on you, would you?" he calls from the other room.

"Whisky?"

"Yeah. You know, fire water? Alcohol? Bug Juice?"

"Oh. Synthahol. Not this very moment, no. If you want some, I can probably bring you some later."

"Do that, would you?"

"Of course. For now, we should really get going, though."

"What am I supposed to be doing when I get there?" He walks back into the room, hair neatly combed and his face freshly washed.

"Huberus will be walking you through your daily duties. You'll be in Beahl's chambers most of the day, and if things go right, in the bridge this evening. While you're there, I need you to find a couple of things for me."

"Okay." One eyebrow rises higher than the other. "What am I supposed to be looking for?"

"One, there should be a special key hidden somewhere in Beahl's quarters. I need it."

"A *special* key," he repeats mockingly.

"Yes. The other thing we need is the remote to our implants."

"What does it look like?"

Here's the tricky part.

"I have no idea. I'm hoping you'll recognize it when you see it. It should be small, will probably fit in the palm of your hand. I suspect it will have several buttons on it, but it might be totally voice-activated. I really don't know. Just be careful with it, and don't press anything in case it—"

He throws his hand in the air, showing me his palm as he glares at me in that special way I think is reserved just for me now.

"Just haud yer wheesht a minute," he growls. "Is yer heid full o'mince?"

"Huh?" I give him a blank stare.

"You mean to tell me that I'm going into a man's hoose to find a little contraption that can kill us all, but we don't have any idea what the gadget actually looks like or where it might be or what buttons I should or should not press?"

That's about the size of it.

"Don't forget the key," I add. "It is vitally important."

He sighs heavily. "If you say so. I guess I don't have any choice but to trust you on that. I might be a total bawheed for this, but let's go."

Besides the house bots, who are busy arranging for morning meals and performing the predawn chores, the hallways are relatively empty. When Bruce isn't gawking at the bots, I take the opportunity to show him a bit of the ship on our way to Beahl's quarters. It might benefit us for him to learn his way around.

"The galley is that way, and the bridge is down there." I

point toward each of the various unmarked corridors as he frowns at me. "Huberus will probably show you the bridge this afternoon."

"What's that?" He jerks his head toward two glinting swords mounted in a crisscross pattern on the wall above the intersection. It's the only unnecessary decoration on the entire vessel, at least outside of Beahl's quarters, and justly confirms the vanity of the ship's owner.

"The DeCombre insignias. Beahl's heraldry," I explain, unable to keep the look of disgust from my face.

"Where I come from, when the swords point upward like that—"

"They're ready for a fight," I finish. "Perhaps we are not so different, after all."

"Maybe not," he says, and we continue on with our little tour.

"The commons are that way," I tell him, pointing down the next corridor. "But, we're going this way."

"I hope you don't plan on quizzing me over all this later," he grumbles.

Despite my usual churlish disposition, I find myself smiling. The resemblance between Bruce and my mate is striking now that I know they're related. I find I actually like this male. To my unending shock, he's kept me laughing most of the morning, and that's not something I've done much of, if at all, since my capture two full rotations ago. Come to think of it, I didn't do much of it before that, either. It makes me wonder if things could always be like this, if I could smile like this all the time. I believe it's possible when I think of my mate. Is this what being happy means?

"Here we are. These are Beahl's quarters," I inform him as we enter.

Bruce steps inside and pauses to take in all the lavish decor. Beahl has a double suite, which may not sound like much, but on a ship where there's never enough space, it's a lot. While Bruce gawks, Huberus hurries toward us from the galley. It's kind of fun watching a droid stress out. He races past the blood red settee that Beahl picked up last cycle on a run to Gishtu and nearly trips over the matching twin ball chairs. Finally, he screeches to a halt in front of us.

"Huberus, this is Bruce Liam MacTavish, the human that Beahl made mention of this morning. Your trainee," I tell him.

Bruce sticks out his hand, palm facing vertically, and says, "Nice to meet you."

Huberus looks at his hand, then back at his face, and then back at his hand again, as though trying to figure out what to do with it. Finally, I guess he decides to ignore it in lieu of a scornful look, which he directs at Bruce this time.

"From now on, human, your name is HS Six Three Seven Two. And, when you greet your master, you will be silent, and bow, like this," he says, bending low at his waist.

Bruce eyes him murderously, I think just now figuring out that Huberus is a droid.

"When I see my *master*, I'll be sure to do that," he says. "Right after I kick his —"

"Airlock!" I shout before he can finish his thought, and he screws up his face and squints.

"Fine," he snaps.

"Wonderful," I reply a little sardonically before turning my attention back to the snooty droid. "Huberus, I'm sure you two have a lot of work to do. You'll see him back to his quarters when you're done?"

"Of course," he says, spinning around and giving me his back.

They're midway into their next lesson when I step out into the hall and close the door behind me. One MacTavish taken care of. Now, to go check on the luscious, red-haired one.

# CHAPTER NINE

Aine

For breakfast, the little food bot—whose name is ES Four Three Nine, according to her—brought me something resembling fluffy scrambled eggs and a roasted leg of krustof, whatever that is. It looked like a chicken drumstick, but it had a hoof attached to it, which didn't do much to promote my appetite. I didn't care, though. I ate it, anyway, every bite of it, needing my strength to escape.

ES Four Three Nine also brought me some hot water and two small bags of something she called teska. It tasted like a mix of tea and apple juice, and I drank every bit of that, too. I hung on to the bags, waited for them to cool, and then I laid back down on my cot, applying one to each of my eyes.

"God, that feels good."

I've resorted to talking to myself since I don't have anyone else to talk to. My lids feel heavy, and my eyes are so puffy, they're almost painful. I barely got a wink of sleep last night.

I reach beside me and grab my fork-chop, which is what I've dubbed my eating utensil. I held on to it this morning, too, after admiring its versatile functionality. Running my fingers up and down the smooth wood-like surface, I test the tip against the pad of my finger. It's the only weapon I have, and it's not quite sharp enough. I'll have to find a way to sharpen it before tonight, since according to at least one of the guards, they're coming back to see me.

A few of them came during the night and decided to

sample some of their merchandise. Maybe I've never been with a man before, but I'm not so innocent that I didn't know what was going on over there. I've seen all kinds of horrible things on Earth, some of it cruel, some even heart-wrenching. I'd be the first to admit that humans are capable of some pretty bad shit, but what I heard last night went beyond disturbing. It was heartless, and one hundred percent subhuman. Even now, my hands shake when I think about the girls' screams.

I don't know if they raped Jill or Celia, or both or neither of them, and I'm not sure I want to know. I am sure they're both traumatized, though. Neither has said a word all morning. Come to think of it, none of them has spoken this morning. That alone says a lot when you consider forty or fifty females all crammed together in a small space like this. I've tried to work up the courage to speak to them, but I just can't do it. I have no idea what to even say, so my silence is my solidarity.

While a couple of the guards were having their fun in the other girls' cells, a few of them were trying to break into mine. I've never seen men, or whatever they are, so damned determined to pick a lock. All I could do was huddle in the corner and pray they wouldn't be successful. It seemed like they worked on that lock for hours, each of them taking a turn or two, before they finally gave up. The especially nasty one called Shan finally threw in the towel just a little while ago, leaving me with his promise to return later with the right tools. And, I've no doubt he intends to keep his word.

The tea, or teska, bags, are working magic helping to soothe my tired, puffy eyes, but there's nothing that can soothe my tattered nerves or the ache in my chest for the other girls. And, dammit, I'll say it. I'm afraid. Fucking terrified. I hate it, but there it is. I'm weak and pathetic and a shivering mess, fighting total despair. And, it's a battle that I'm currently losing.

My only real hope right now is Griz, and I haven't even seen him since yesterday. Still, I can't put too much stock in him as a solution since he's just a slave, like me, and probably in the same boat. Though, he's not under threat of rape every second of the day and night when we're all at the mercy of our captors. Doesn't matter, anyway. He's probably forgotten all about me by now. Did he even remember to tell Bruce that I'm here?

Sitting up on the edge of my cot, I let the fake tea bags fall into my lap and stare at my bare feet while the fork-chop rolls back and forth between my palms. I have to decide what I'm going to do. Granted, my options are pretty limited — either give in to the inevitable and hope they don't hurt me too bad. Or, fight the bastards knowing they'll take me, anyway. There's no way I can protect myself from even one of them, much less two or three, but I think I'd rather die fighting.

Well, honestly, I'd rather not die at all. I'd rather come up with a good plan to escape. My only chance is to run if Shan gets my cell door open, and I've no doubt that he will. Maybe I could take him by surprise? I could lie very still like I'm asleep or terrified, which wouldn't be difficult because I would be, and then stab him in the eye with my fork-chop once he's close enough. But then, where would I even escape to? I'm on a freaking spaceship in the middle of space. The best I could do is find a little hole, maybe crawl inside, and try to hide.

I abandon my thoughts as the now-familiar clanking of keys brings several gasps from the prisoners, myself included. Flinching, I grasp at my blanket and drag it over myself. Are they back so soon? I'm not ready yet. My heart pounds with every footstep, and I clutch my fork-chop in a death grip beneath the blanket. I expect to see Shan's cold, reptilian face appear any second, but thank the heavens, that's not who shows up.

"Griz!"

Immediately, I'm on my feet, bolting toward the bars.

His appearance alone triggers an avalanche of emotion, and I'm bawling again before I know it. I reach for him desperately through the bars like the pathetic victim I don't want to be. I don't even know why. He rushes to me, flattening himself against the bars and wrapping his hands over mine.

"Aine, what is it? What's wrong, my little warrior?"

"Little warrior?" I hiccup and wipe my eyes against my shoulder. "Not hardly."

"Why are your eyes leaking like this?"

The look he gives me is priceless, and I can't help but laugh. Unfortunately, I sob at the same time, so it comes out more like a snort. I shake my head. What's the point in even telling him about something he can't do anything about?

"I have to get out of here," I tell him instead. "Today."

Worry lines crease his forehead, and he reaches a tentative finger to wipe a stray tear from my cheek.

"Tell me. Tell me what's happened."

The softness is gone from his voice, and it's like my tongue is compelled to respond.

"The guards came again this morning," I blurt, lowering my head and taking an abnormal interest in my pink toenail polish.

He grips my chin and raises my face so I have to look at him. "Did they hurt you?"

Not trusting myself to speak, I shake my head.

"Only them," I say, jerking my head toward Jill's cell and trying to stop my lip from trembling.

Griz takes a deep breath and reaches around me, pulling me into a welcome hug. Well, as much of a hug as he can with three-inch iron bars in between us. Still, his touch sends a tingling sensation throughout my body, and I feel braver, stronger just from being in his arms.

"Frizzucking bastards," he grumbles as he places a soft kiss on top of my head and gently strokes my hair. "It'll be alright, my princess."

"He said he was coming back tonight, Griz. He said he was bringing tools with him to unlock my door," I tell him, my voice so small and shaky, I almost don't recognize it.

Stepping back, he grips my shoulders tightly as he leans down to put his face close to mine. "Who? Who said that?"

"The guard," I sniff. "The one called Shan."

Griz's face hardens, and I swear I can see murder in his eyes.

"Shan," he repeats, and I nod.

"I have to get out of here. Or, just bring me a knife or something, anything I can use to protect myself," I plead. Then, I remember Lionese's visit. "Can you get to one of those fuzzy rope things they wear on their belts?"

He looks at me strangely. "A welter whip? What do you know of those?"

"I know they hurt like Hell," I scoff.

"He whipped you?" Griz growls, and I flinch away from his seething anger. Immediately, he relaxes his grip on my arms and strokes me lightly with his thumbs. "Don't be afraid of me, amavi. I would never hurt you."

I know he wouldn't. I nod and give him a weak smile.

"Now, tell me. Did Shan whip you?" he asks again, softer this time, but I can see the muscles working in his jaw.

"Not him. A different one. I think his name was Lionese. Is there any way you can get ahold of one?"

He doesn't answer right away. He just stands there breathing heavily, his chest rising and falling like he's about to implode. He's starting to scare me again.

"Griz," I say softly, reaching out to touch his face. "Can you help me? All I have is a fork-chop, and somehow, I don't think that's going to be enough."

"A fork-chop?"

"Yeah," I reply, stepping back to my cot and picking up my chopstick fork to wave it at him, then make a little stabbing motion so he gets the gist. "This thing. I don't know if I could actually kill anyone with it, though. I need something better to fight him with, something more than a little stick with a dull tip."

He sighs heavily. "Aine, come here."

I do as he says, stepping back to the bars and pressing my face against them.

"Listen to me, amavi," he says, cupping my cheeks. "Do not worry. I will take care of Shan. He will not bother you again. I promise."

"What are you going to do?" I mean, really. He's just a slave, too. Right?

"Let me worry about that. Just trust me. Please."

The look he gives me nearly melts my insides, and for some reason I can't explain, I know I do trust him. Even with my life.

"I do trust you," I whisper.

I see the approval in his eyes, and he leans forward to seal his promise with a light kiss to my lips. It's not lustful, not sexual in the least, but it's still the best damn kiss I've ever had in my life. The tattoo of my heart thrums in my ears, and my toes curl as his breath spreads warmth throughout me, erasing any doubts and filling me with a courage and confidence I've never experienced before. I blink my eyes open and stare at him, dumbfounded.

He gives me a cocky smile, and the spell is suddenly broken. Poof. Just like that. He obviously knows I'm attracted to him, and I'd laugh if I wasn't so weirded out.

"Your sire says to tell you hello and that he loves you," he says sweetly.

I gasp, unable to contain my happiness. "Really? Where is

he? Is he still okay?"

"He is fine, sweetling. He's being held in one of the guest quarters on the other side of the ship."

"Is there any way I can see him?"

Griz's smile disappears, and he looks at me sadly. There's no need for him to reply. I can already see the answer in his eyes.

"Soon, amavi. I promise."

"Okay," I reply, forcing a smile. "At least he's safe and sober, I guess."

"Actually, he's asked me to bring him some synthahol. Does he drink often?"

"You could say that." I snort again. "He didn't use to, though."

He gives me a sympathetic squeeze. "I know a lot of mackis who've made the mistake of trying to drown their sorrows in synthahol. It never works. I'll try to make another check on him tonight just to be sure he's all right."

"Thank you, Griz. I appreciate that," I tell him wholeheartedly, rewarding him with a real smile this time. *Damn, he's handsome.*

"I understand the love for a sire," he says. "I lost mine many rotations ago."

"I'm sorry." I squeeze his fingers. "What about your mum?"

He clenches his jaw and lowers his head as if in shame. "Beahl has my dam. He took her after the last time I tried to escape, and gave her to someone on Janyx. He said it's the best way to make sure I 'behave' and follow orders. As far as I know, everyone thinks we're dead."

"Oh my god." My eyes fill with fluid. "I wish . . . I wish there was something I could do, Griz."

"I will save her," he says, gazing into my eyes so I can see the truth of his words. "And, I will save you and your sire, too."

I almost believe it. He seems bigger than life, like there's nothing he can't do. And, from the moment I first met him, there's just been something about him, something drawing me to him like a moth to a flame. I've never felt anything like it.

He leans back away from the bars to do a quick scan of the corridor, making sure we're still alone. Then, he presses his face to the bars and whispers in my ear. "Three days, Aine. We leave here in three days."

I gasp, and he shushes me.

"I have a plan. It will work. I know it will."

"Tell me," I demand, and he does.

For the next ten minutes, I listen intently, hanging on to every word.

Done now, he reaches his finger between the bars, places it beneath my chin, and pushes closed my gaping maw.

"Can you do this, my brave princess? Are you truly willing to fight for your freedom?"

"Yes," I tell him unreservedly, my fists already clenching. "Hell, yes. I will fight."

He smiles. "Three days, then. Remember, good things come to those who help themselves."

"Wait," I correct him out of habit.

"Yes? What is it?" he asks, and suddenly, I feel like I'm performing a Laurel and Hardy routine.

"No," I say, biting my lip to keep from laughing, my heart warming toward him even more. "Good things come to those who *wait*."

"Are you sure? That's not what Bruce said."

I snort again with laughter. I can't help it. Then, it's my turn to lean forward and kiss Griz. Like him, I start off soft and subtle. But when I feel his hands close around my waist and crush me to him, I am totally lost.

Suddenly, I'm totally surrounded by Griz's presence. He's

everywhere all at once, filling up all my senses, consuming me. My breath hitches as he tugs at the thin material of my dress, roughly swiping it aside and exposing my breasts. A ragged, guttural purr rumbles in his chest as he breaks our kiss and stares at me hungrily.

"Mine," he growls, and liquid heat coils low in my belly.

My nipples pebble beneath his penetrating gaze, and he brushes them with his thumbs, coaxing them into hard points and squeezing them hard enough to rip a groan from my throat. Leaning forward, he takes one in his mouth, nipping and suckling. My knees buckle, and if he wasn't holding me up, I'd be dissolved into a squishy pool on the floor.

"Griz," I whimper, my hands fisting in his hair.

He releases me with a pop and a final brush of his tongue.

"You are mine, amavi," he says as his unrelenting gaze causes me to gush in excitement. "This is mine," he informs me, squeezing my breast in his rough, calloused hand. "And, this, amavi. This is mine, too. *Only* mine."

He reaches beneath my dress and drags his warm fingers through my soaking wet folds, spreading my juices back and forth. I tremble, my breath ragged and choppy as his fingers lightly circle my clit.

"Only I will bring you this kind of pleasure. Do you understand?"

I mewl some kind of response as I bury my face in his neck. I've never been so turned on, never been so wet or felt anything so incredible. Until he pinches my clit, squeezing it firmly between his fingers as delicious waves of pleasure roll through me over and over again. I come harder than I've ever come in my life. I have to bite down on his shoulder to keep from screaming as stars dance across my eyelids. Finally, I sag against him, wobbling and boneless from the aftershocks.

"Amavi," Griz whispers in awe as I lie there slobbering against his shoulder, trying to recover my senses. "You have marked me."

Huh? I raise my head to look, and am appalled by my teeth marks in the valley between his neck and shoulders. Sweet baby Jane. He's bleeding!

"Oh my god." I look at him with wide eyes, horrified at my political incorrectness. "I am so sorry, Griz. That must have hurt."

You'd never know it by his radiant smile, though. He buries his face in my neck, scraping his fangs against my tender skin. "Amavi. You have marked me. I am yours. And, I will claim you, too. As soon as we are free, I will claim what is already mine."

I can't speak yet. I just stand there trying to comprehend his latest revelation while he removes his hand from beneath my dress. He pushes his fingers into his mouth, sucking shamelessly as my maw gapes wide again. His eyes drift shut as he savors them. Then, he removes them with a pop, kisses me one more time, and pulls the pieces of my gown back together. "I'll be back as soon as I can."

I nod, still in a half-swoon, and watch as he walks away.

What the fuck just happened?

# Chapter Ten

Griz

I practically strut down the hallway, the memory of my mate's sweet face as she orgasmed by my hand filling me with renewed purpose and adding a swagger to my steps. She claimed me! My fingers rub against her mark, and I smile, wanting to roar my claim to the entire ship. But I don't dare. Not yet.

The scent of Aine's arousal lingers all around me, her taste still fresh on my tongue. One stroke of my finger against her soft, wet folds, and I came in my pants like a randy fledgling. One finger! I can hardly imagine the bliss that awaits when I finally claim her with my cock. The thought of it makes me hard again already.

And her kisses. Sweet Goddess! The way she licked my fangs. I ache for her like I've never ached for anyone or anything. Even though I've just had release, I'm hard as Votunbaerg stone again at the mere thought of claiming her. My body trembles as I picture it, Aine naked on her hands and knees, spread before me like a submissive feast as I take the sweet gift of her innocence and make her mine forever.

Frizzuck! I have to stop this before I come in my pants again. It's not like I've never had a femki before. I haven't saved myself as she has, never believing I even had an amavi compar, much less expecting to ever find her. Even so, I've never been tempted to claim anyone. Not until now.

All my life, I've heard the mackis on Tarilax speak of the

intensity of a true claiming and the unbelievable bliss of the mating lock. I never fully understood until now. I know I won't be able to stop the mating lock once I finally take her. It will be too strong to resist. My instincts will take over, over-riding my will as soon as my fangs sink into her soft, pale skin and my cock strikes home, nestled in my mate's beautiful pussy.

Already, I long to have her in my arms again, and have to fight the urge to turn around and go back. At least, she looked sated and well-satisfied when I left. Her eyes weren't nearly as puffy and had stopped leaking. I did not care for that at all. How dare that lecherous Lizentine piece of shiest, Shan, threaten my mate and cause her eyes to leak. He isn't even fit to breathe the same air as my princess. And, Lionese . . . . A growl rumbles in me, and my pace quickens. He, too, will be made to pay. No one strikes my amavi and lives.

My erection deflates like a punctured balloon at the thought of the males who've hurt my mate. Now's not a good time to be distracted by a stiff cock, anyway, not when I'm in search of prey. Shan will be the first to taste my vengeance. The bastard's already dead. He just doesn't know it yet.

As I near the commons, I glance up at the gaudy swords that decorate the wall. Only a prideful idiot would place weapons in such easy reach of his slaves and enemies. I stretch out my hand and grasp one of the swords, tugging it gently to loosen it from its scabbard. It doesn't budge, so I pull harder until it finally gives. The sword sings as it leaves its nesting spot, the metal chinking in a familiar way that makes my warrior blood heat with excitement.

Sword in hand, I walk quickly toward the commons before anyone sees me, gripping the hilt of the blade tightly, weigh-ing it, and trying to get a feel for its awkward size. Pausing at the maintenance closet just outside, I palm the security scan-ner on the wall. As a slave, my prints won't open many doors on the ship, but a maintenance closet poses no problem. The door slides open with a whoosh, and I lean the sword against the inside wall, hoping that none of the house bots or servants find it before I get back. I'm ready now.

Ignoring the big wet spot at the front of my leggings, I re-arrange myself and prepare to enter the commons. It's where Beahl's soldiers go to gather and drink, usually right before many of them make their way down to the femkis' cells for their evening entertainment.

On Tarilax, no macki would dream of harming a femki. The penalty for raping or causing intentional injury to a femki is swift death, not that anyone needs that kind of deterrent. We treat our femkis like the goddesses they are, and the thought of these mongrels touching any of them enrages me. The thought of them touching my *mate* drives me into a blind, murderous craze.

I step inside the noisy room and inventory my surroundings. I haven't been here in a long time, but it looks the same — a few scuffed tables, some unidentifiable stains on the carpet, and a well-stocked bar in the back. Several Lizentine soldiers camp at the bar, along with a few of the mercs from Rana and a good portion of the cargo crew. That's good. It's crowded enough that I can blend right in. So that's where I head first.

"Greetings, Tarilean. I am Jep, your bartender. What'll you have?" The bar bot wipes the counter in front of me with a dirty towel.

"Shot of kocho," I tell him. "On second thought, bring the bottle."

Jep scurries away to fill my order, and I focus on the task at hand, tuning into the various conversations taking place throughout the room, inspecting the occupants in the smoky mirror that hangs behind the bar. With any luck, my target will already be here, well on his way to inebriation, and I won't have long to wait.

Moments later, Jep returns with an empty shot glass and a bottle of kocho, the cheap kind. He's pouring me a glass before I can even get my credit chip out of my pocket.

"Keep the change," I tell him, and not for the first time, wonder what an AI uses its tips for. It probably all goes back into Beahl's pocket.

I pound the kocho quickly, reveling in the burn as it slides down my throat. Then, I pour myself another and sip on it slowly while I wait. From the corner of my eye, I sight a familiar face, a Lizentine guard I've seen often hanging around with Shan.

"Where's your pal tonight, Balda?" one of the Rana mercs asks him.

Balda gives his shoulder a shrug. "I'm sure he'll be along. Lionese had us polishing steel all day."

The merc laughs. "You guys in trouble again?"

Balda curses under his breath before finishing off his ale. "There he is. Shan! Over here!"

I glance at the mirror and spy the wretched guard, Shan, ambling toward us. My fangs ache to rip out his throat, but I must be patient. I have to wait for the right time. I grit my teeth as he approaches, watching while he slaps his slimy cohorts on the back and plants himself between them at the bar.

Their laughter echoes through my hollow veins, and I catch myself just before my iron grip shatters the shot glass in my hand. This swine thinks to molest my mate? I am more than ready to deliver a subtle reminder of Tarilean justice. In fact, I vibrate with the need.

Instead, I swipe the bottle off the bar and stuff it beneath my arm, slipping outside to put some distance between us. If I stay in here, I won't be able to stop myself from killing him in front of everyone. So, I go back to the maintenance closet and wait.

It doesn't take long for Shan to stumble out, and as I feared, his Lizentine friend is with him. I almost feel shame for what I'm about to do, but an honorable fight is simply not possible. Honor is a luxury I can't afford right now. I'd love nothing more than to challenge him, to kill him slowly and painfully with a righteous sword and vindicate my mate as she deserves. But my mate's safety is at stake, and there's no low I won't stoop to in order to protect her.

I lurk just inside the closet, watching as they approach, and as soon as they're close enough, I reach out and grab Shan's collar, jerking him inside with me. Before he even knows what's happening, I spear him through the chest and toss his limp body to the floor behind me.

The Lizentine is shocked for a split-click, but recovers quickly. "Why, you —"

He lunges for me, but I'm ready for him. I feint left then dodge to the right, using my momentum to pull him into the closet while I swing the blade at the same time. I feel it slice neatly through the tendons in his neck as he slingshots past me. Then, his head makes a squishy sound as it glides off his shoulders and falls to the floor with a meaty thump to land beside his friend. I find, to my surprise, that Shan is still alive, staring horrified into Balda's lifeless eyes. Good.

"Shan," I say, my voice icy.

"Please," he begs, fat drops of black blood seeping from his lips. "Don't."

It's good that he's alive, that he's begging for his life. It brings me an enormous amount of satisfaction that I can tell him why he is dying today. The closet is very small, and it only takes a couple of steps before I'm towering over him.

"Do you know why you're about to die, Lizentine?"

He whimpers pathetically and shakes his head. "No. Don't, please."

"Is that what the femkis said last night when you were raping them in their cells? Tell me, Shan, did you show them any mercy?"

He says nothing, trying to scoot away from me, but his foot slips and slides in the growing pool of blood.

"I will show you the same mercy that you showed them. Did you really think I would allow you to harm my mate?"

"Mate? I didn't—" His voice fails as he shakes his head in desperation.

"I should have killed you long ago. Just know that you die now because you have no honor and no decency. Go and join your friend in Haelic."

"Tarilean, stop—" He gasps as I raise the sword.

But I don't stop, opting instead to plunge it deep into the other side of his chest, through his thick, already blood-stained scales and straight into his second, black heart.

I could have drawn it out, made it more painful. He probably deserved to suffer more for the injuries he's inflicted on those helpless femkis, not to mention those he would no doubt have inflicted on my mate. In a way, I showed him mercy he did not merit. Too bad I couldn't fight them both properly and kill them the way a true warrior should. I have to be satisfied with just the knowledge that they can't hurt Aine, and that's enough for me.

I drag their bodies to the corner and do my best to cover them with old sheets, cleaning cloths and a busted laundry cart. Then, I mop up the blood and stuff the towels deep into an old barrel of cleaning solution. It's just a matter of time before they're found, but they only have to stay hidden until we get to Kerberos. Only two more days, and we'll be there.

After wiping down the blade, I stuff it inside a food trolley and exit quickly before I'm spotted by any of the other crew entering or leaving the commons. I make my way quickly back toward Bruce's quarters, only pausing long enough to replace the sword back into its original sheath. I ditch the trolley around the next corner and finally arrive at Bruce's door.

"Haud Yer Wheesht!" he shouts from inside when I knock again.

His door swings wide, and I'm relieved to see that he has his pants on this time. I don't wait to be invited in. Instead, I muscle past him, kicking the door closed behind me.

"Care to come in?" he asks sardonically.

"So?" I ask impatiently, forgetting all manner of manners. "Did you find the remote?"

He scowls and eyes me warily. "It wasn't in his room."

"Shieska!" We can't leave without that remote. At least, not unless I can find a way to disarm and remove the implants. "What about the key? Did you find the key?"

"Maybe," he says stubbornly. "Just what does this key do exactly?"

I take a deep breath, scrambling for patience. This is my mate's sire, due my trust and respect. "It opens Aine's cell. I hope."

His eyes widen.

"Take me to her," he demands in his haughty human way.

"It won't do you any good. Even if you got her out of the cell, where would you go? Just trust me. I'm going to get us out of here."

"Trust you? T'aint no easy feat to trust a man with blood on his hands."

What? I look down to see that I do, in fact, still have blood on my hands.

"Pardon me while I use your refresher," I say, refusing to acknowledge anything.

As I wash my hands for the third time, I consider Bruce's stubbornness. He may just need a little persuading.

When I'm done, I walk to the small mini-galley in the back of the apartment and grab two cups. Then, I return to my mate's headstrong sire and give him a polite bow.

"Thank you, distinguished sire of mi amavi compar. And,

my apologies. I forgot to give this to you before." I pull the bottle of kocho from my pocket and watch as his face lights up. "Perhaps this will help with your trust issues?"

"Oh, it will. I'm sure it will," he agrees, licking his lips as he reaches for the bottle.

I jerk the bottle back, shaking my head and holding out my empty hand in its place. "Key first."

# CHAPTER ELEVEN

Bruce

Blast! I can't do it. I can't betray my kin, my own lovely daughter. This key might be our only way out, but I really do need that drink. For two days, my guts have been in a twist, and I can't keep the tremble from my hands. Just one little sip would help. It would take the edge off my nerves and clear out some of the fog so I can think. Right now, the only thing I can think about is drinking. Or, fighting. Or, drinking and fighting. Maybe fecking, too. But, I ken that none of these things will help Aine right now. I'm a sorry excuse for a father.

The alien wants me to trust him. Says he's going to escape and take me and my Aine with him. Now, why would he do that? Out of the goodness of his heart, I suppose? Does he think I'm some sort of a fud or a simpleton? I give him a hard look, but I still can't find a single trace of malice in the guy. So, why, then? It's got me totally buggered.

"Tell you what," I finally say as I scratch my stubbly chin with flicking fingers. "What say we sit down over here and have ourselves a little craic?"

"A little what?"

I chuckle as he tilts his head, and his face takes on that blank expression that I like so much.

"Chat. Let's have us a chat," I tell him, already making my way over to the little sitting area. I watch, amused, as he folds his huge body into a chair that was obviously never meant to support a man of his size and girth. My eyes drift down to the flagon in his hand, and his fingers tighten around the bottle's neck.

"What would you like to chat about?" he asks with an air of confidence I can tell he doesn't really feel.

I may be the one with the shakes, but he's sure as shite the one with the nerves right now. I keep my withering stare on him, and before long, he begins to twitch. They always do. He thinks to ply me with whisky in exchange for my key and all my secrets. He almost succeeded, but thoughts of my family will keep me strong in my purpose. I'd never betray them, never betray Aine.

"Why don't you pour us both a little swallow of that bevvy, and it might loosen my tongue a bit," I tell him.

He smirks, but I can tell he's debating.

"One little swallow," he finally says, and places two empty cups on the small table between us.

My mouth waters in anticipation as the mysterious brown elixir splashes against the sides the cup. Then, he pours a second one and hands it to me. My hand shakes as I take it from him, bringing it straight to my lips and downing it in one gulp.

"Ahh," I manage to get out before the burning in my throat renders my vocal cords pretty much useless. I doubt diesel fuel could be any harsher. "What is that stuff?" I croak.

The alien laughs and takes a small sip from his own cup. "It's called kocho, and it's got a kick to it. I was going to warn you, but you didn't give me time."

"What's your plan here, alien? Are you trying to get me to do your dirty work?"

"What? I . . . No!"

"You plan to sneak out of here and leave me holding the bag?"

"Of course not! You . . . I mean, Aine. I need — "

"You're gonna let Aine take the blame?"

The damn alien doesn't even try to answer that one. He just starts growling like a Rottweiler.

"What's your interest in my daughter? Spit it out, lad."

He stops growling and gives me that blank look again. It's all I can do not to cackle.

You don't live the kind of life I have and not pick up a trick or two. I've learned that being blunt and throwing rapid curve balls out of left field often takes an opponent off-guard. If you can rile him up enough, he'll sometimes start blurting, more often than not, the truth.

"What are you trying to pull, E.T.? You think you're going to diddle my daughter?"

Oh, shite. Suddenly, the enormous seven-foot-tall alien in the chair across from me seems to expand right before my very eyes. His tawny color turns dark, and he dons a champion scowl, even better than mine, I think. I swear his fangs get longer, and the veins in his neck strain against his skin. What was in that drink? I may have pushed him a little too hard.

"No one will be 'diddling' Aine," he roars as he flies up out of his chair, and I nearly shite myself.

"Calm down, you loon. We're just having a chat." He seems to get hold of himself a wee bit. Though, his chest still heaves in and out a little harder than makes me comfortable. "Just sit down and pour us another swallow to calm our nerves."

Ah. There's that blank look again. I see the corner of his mouth twitch, but he does it. He sits down and pours us both another cup of diesel fuel. My hand is a little steadier this time as I reach for it.

"There's a good lad," I tell him as I take a small sip. "Now, why don't we cut through all the shite, and you tell me what's going on. I ken you're not a bad fella'."

Finally, the bullshite persona melts away, and I'm staring at the truth face to face.

"Aine is my amavi compar," he tells me. "My fated mate."

"Your—"

"Fated mate, yes. I've known it since the first time I saw her. She is destined to walk beside me in this life and in the hereafter. She is my true partner, and I hers. We were made by the Goddess for one another."

"Uh huh," I squint at him as I take another sip from my cup. "Does she know this?"

"I have told her that she is mine, yes."

"And she didn't hand you your arse?"

"If by that you mean she didn't flay me, then that's correct. I believe, deep down, she knows this truth, as well."

"Uh huh." I nod, my entire body numb either from the kocho or the shock of some nimrod telling me he's my daughter's fated husband.

"Don't worry," he blurts. "I have not yet claimed her."

My arsehole suddenly shrivels to the size of a small pea, and my eyes dart around the room searching for something sharp to kill him with.

"Bruce . . . honored sire. I know that Aine is a princess back on your Earth," he starts.

There! I can use that ice pick thingie.

" . . . And I am but the cousin of a king. However, I vow to love and cherish her all the days of her life, and I pledge my sword, my honor and my life to defend her. Nothing will harm her so long as I live."

My eyebrows rise up an inch or two. Something he says catches my interest, and I decide to let him live another minute or two. I take a long draw of kocho and roll my eyes over him slowly.

"Cousin of a king, you say?"

"I am Grizolde Theodosius Ja'Lento, honored guard of the

Tarilean king, and third in line to the throne of Tarilax. Could you ever accept my claim as your daughter's honored fated mate?"

I pick up my cup and drain it, never taking my eyes from his. Then, I hold it out and shake it at him, a silent indication for him to fill it back up. He does. Bless him.

Sadness fills me as I take another drink of the kocho. I knew this day would come. The day some man, or . . . er . . . male, would sweep in and take my bonny little lass away from me. It doesn't make it any easier, though.

"You'd protect her with your life? I have your word on it?"

"On my honor, sire. I will protect your daughter with my dying breath."

By God, I believe he would. I nod my agreement. "Then, I'll give you her hand."

The lad wilts like a hot-house lily in August, and then, a near-blinding smile breaks out on his face.

"Thank you. Thank you, sire. You will never be sorry. I swear it."

"Hold on, now, lad. I'm saying *only* if she wants you. You understand?"

My condition doesn't seem to dampen his happiness one iota. "Perfectly."

"Now, tell me how you're going to get her out of here."

He draws a deep breath and exhales loudly. "In two spans time, we'll be stopping on Kerberos so Beahl can steal more females. I had thought to find the remote and deactivate our implants tomorrow. Then, after we've arrived on Kerberos, I planned to unlock Aine's cell and have you collect her. I've already prepared an exit for the two of you. But now . . . ." He shakes his head and drains the rest of his kocho. "We'll have to find a way to deactivate the implants directly."

"That's not a bad plan," I tell him, picking up the bottle and refilling both our cups.

"It isn't," he agrees. "But, without the remote, we're stuck."

"Not necessarily." I give him my best shite-eating grin. "I told you I didn't find the remote in his quarters, and that's true. It was actually on the bridge."

The edges of his mouth curl up, and he has a fairly decent shite-eating grin, too.

"Can we steal it?" he asks.

"Steal it? I don't know about that, but I'm fairly certain I can deactivate it."

"How?"

"Look, alien. You've got your gifts, and I've got mine. I was a Master Electrician on Earth. If it's got wires, I can fix it. Or, break it, whatever the situation calls for. The problem will be clearing the room long enough for me to do it."

He wrinkles his forehead and stares unseeing over my shoulder, obviously lost in thought. I take advantage of the opportunity to study my new son-in-law-to-be. I think Aine's mum would approve. Lachlin, too. All I can do is use my best judgement since neither is here to weigh in. But, I think it's what a good father would do. He may be a slave today, but he won't be for much longer. He loves her, that much is obvious. We're in a strange universe, one which he's obviously mastered. She needs him. And, finally, my Aine will officially become royalty, as she's always deserved to be.

"I've got it," he says calmly. "I'll create a diversion."

"How?"

"Dead bodies. I'll pull them into the corridor."

"You're just going to go out and kill some random folks to create a diversion?" Feck! Maybe I was wrong about this guy, after all.

"No." He laughs. "Don't be silly. They're already dead. I killed them on the way over here."

"What the feck?" I nearly shite myself again.

"No! You don't understand," he says, trying to calm me.

"They were going to hurt Aine. I had to."

That got my attention. I place my half-full glass on the table and sit forward in my seat as I look him squarely in the eye.

"Tell me," I demand. "Tell me everything."

# CHAPTER TWELVE

Aine

There's a weird little dust bunny attached to the corner of my cell that flaps and flutters at random times throughout the day and catches my eye whenever I fall restless or still, which is most of the time. I stare at it a lot.

Now, it dances in the dim light from the hallway, trapped in place by some unknown force or circumstance, like it's struggling to break free. Space dust? I laugh out loud. That's exactly what I feel like right now. Space dust. A tiny speck of DNA blowing around in an infinite universe. I was attached to Earth for a while. Now, I'm attached to this ship, trapped and struggling to break free. *I'm attached to Griz now. "Mine," he said.* I shake my head, reluctant to go there right now.

I spent most of the evening thinking about Griz. It's got to be after midnight by now, and I'm still trying to figure out what the hell happened. One minute I was so terrified I was physically sick, and the next minute, I was caught up in the throes of *la petite mort* so hot and tight that I wouldn't have cared if the entire ship melted around us. In fact, I'm surprised it didn't.

I chuckle to myself. Why not? I'm batshit crazy, anyway. How else can I explain this weird thing between me and Griz? I just met him, and yet, I've known him all my life. My body knows him. He owns my orgasms. Hell, he owns me. It's like I've dreamed about him every night, but didn't know it until the minute I saw his face. When he's with me, I feel like I can take on the guards with no problem, the whole ship, even. Bring it on, alien assholes. But when he's gone, I feel the loss. Deeply. It's like a vital piece of me is missing, and I start doubting everything. When did I start needing him?

A loud noise at the end of the hall sends my heart racing. I freeze, listening intently while clutching my fork-chop, a cold sweat forming above my brow. There's only silence now. Finally, I release the breath I didn't realize I was holding. It was just one of the girls. I know this, but any second, I still expect to see Shan and his cohorts striding up the corridor with a blowtorch and a giant lock pick. Griz promised that Shan wouldn't bother me anymore. "Trust me," he said. I'm trying to, but it's really hard.

I'm exhausted. My body is ready to shut down, but my brain is working extra duty, conjuring up every terrifying scenario it can to keep my stomach tied in knots. Forcing my eyes closed, I urge the peacefulness of sleep to take me, and just when I'm convinced it's no use, it finally does.

*Clink. Clang. Ping. Whir. Clink. Clang. Ping. Whir.* I yawn sleepily, stretching so hard that even my toenails strain.

"Good morning, ES Four Three Nine," I mutter sleepily.

I open my eyes and smile at her, not because I'm happy from a good night's sleep, but because I'm happy to finally be awake. Awake and away from all the horrible, grotesque nightmares that plagued me all night long. Even so, there was no sign of Shan. I'll take the nightmares any day of the week. I'm suddenly more grateful to Griz than I'll ever be able to convey, and my smile takes on new meaning.

"Good morning, Prisoner Eight Four Six Nine Two. This morning, we have two Benskin eggs served over bledston toast with a side of grilled gruxton," she reports as she displays my food tray proudly.

"Mm." I exaggerate my excitement as I pad over to the bars to collect my breakfast. "Tell me, ES Four Three Nine. If I'm a prisoner here, a slave, then why do they feed me so well?"

Her top half swivels toward me, which looks weird since her bottom half is still pointed at the food cart in the other direction. I have to concentrate hard on her response because one of her marble eyes keeps floating around in its socket again. It's very distracting.

"Prisoner Eight Four Six Nine Two is destined for Janyx, to be auctioned as a pleasure giver," she replies as if that should clear up any confusion.

"Yeah. So . . ." I pick up my tray and pop a piece of gruxton in my mouth, nearly orgasming as the delicious spicy meat explodes across my taste buds.

"Prisoner Eight Four Six Nine Two must be salubrious and robust by the time we reach Janyx. She must be in top physical order to ensure maximum bids."

"Oh. I see. You're trying to fatten me up like a hog going to market."

"This does not translate," she informs me with a hint of regret in her voice.

I sigh. "Never mind. I understand."

Her top half spins around to line up with her feet, and she glides back to her cart. "Have a nice day, Prisoner Eight Four Six Nine Two."

"You, too, ES Four Three Nine. Oh! Wait!"

She stops, swivels only her neck this time as she rolls her eye at me. "Yes, Prisoner Eight Four Six Nine Two?"

"If you really want me in top condition by the time we reach Janyx, I need to bathe. Any chance I can grab a shower somewhere?"

*Clink. Clang. Ping. Whir. Clink. Clang. Ping. Whir.*

"I will relay the request to Master," she says, and then leaves me to my breakfast.

Who is Master? Probably that Beahl guy. It's not really that

I'm so keen on a shower. Granted, it would be nice, but if I can just get out of this cell, see the rest of the ship, maybe I can come up with a better plan.

Chatter from the other cells has me optimistic that the girls are recovering from the other night's ordeal. I listen while I eat, trying to pick out Jill or Celia from the rest of the prattle. When I'm done eating, I walk over to the bars and slide my tray through the bottom. Then, I press my face against them and take a shot at communicating.

"Hello? Jill? Celia? Anyone?"

"What? Are you afraid we left?"

Even Celia's mocking tone is welcome at this point.

I almost ask if they're all right, but I stop myself just in time. Of course they're not all right. None of us is all right.

"We need to come up with a plan. We can't just can't give up. We have to fight."

It's quiet for a moment, and I'm about to try again when Jill speaks up.

"I'm in," Jill says decidedly, and I sigh with relief.

"If you've got any bright ideas, I'm all ears," Celia replies in her catty tone.

"There's got to be some sort of emergency escape pods somewhere. We have to find them," I tell her. "Surely, there's enough women over there to overwhelm one or two guards when they come back again. We need to take their weapons and keys."

"First of all, that's easy for you to say since you're sitting over there all safe and snug. We're the ones risking our necks. Secondly, I think you've been watching too many episodes of *Star Trek*. What makes you so sure there's even anything remotely similar to an escape pod onboard?"

I can't take any more of Celia's negativity. As if I don't feel guilty enough about being separated. I certainly don't need her rubbing my nose in it.

"Because there has to be," I snap. "Because, otherwise, we're stuck here. That's why. If you don't want to help us, Celia, that's fine. You can just stay here. But, come hell or high water, I'm carrying my ass out of here."

Immediately, I regret speaking so harshly to her. Then, I get angry at myself for feeling bad about snapping at the saucy bitch. She deserved it. I sigh. Whether she deserved it or not, I'd never leave her behind. I'm about to tell her so when she speaks first.

"Well, we need to know that before we do anything else. And, don't forget, if we do find a pod, someone has to actually fly it out of here."

Smiling, I lean my head against the bars and say a quick prayer of thanks. Maybe she's actually coming around.

"You've been talking a lot to that weird robot chick who brings our food. Can you ask her?" Jill suggests hopefully.

"No. I don't think she'll tell me, and she'd run straight back and inform her 'master,' whoever that is. We can't take that chance."

"What an evil bitch," Celia snarks.

"She can't help it. She's made that way. She's actually really nice, for a robot."

"How is that you can understand her?"

"I honestly don't know."

"What about your boyfriend? Don't think we didn't hear you two last night." Celia chuckles, her voice almost playful.

"What? Are you serious?"

"Hell, girl, I'd be surprised if everyone on the ship didn't hear you."

"Whatever. Griz is not my boyfriend," I say, flushing and feeling like I'm in junior high school again. "Still, I'll ask him the next time I see him. Definitely. What about the other girls?"

"What about them?" Jill and Celia ask at the same time.

"Is there any way you can communicate the plan to them? I mean, if we're going to take down the guards, we'll need everyone's help."

"We can try," Jill says. "Some of them aren't overly friendly, though."

"But, surely, they all want to be free? We don't have to be buddies, but we do have to work together if we want to get out of here. Maybe one of them even knows how to fly an escape pod?"

"We'll do it," Celia agrees, and I finally feel like we're making progress.

I retreat to my cot and sit down, hoping beyond hope that Griz shows up soon so I can ask about the pods. *Sure, that's why.* I smirk at my empty cell. Until then, I busy myself by watching my favorite dust bunny.

# Chapter Thirteen

Griz

I show up at Aine's cell early, before my official slave duties are scheduled to begin. Otherwise, I may not be able to see her at all, and that is simply not acceptable. Today will be busy, though. I must make preparations for the raid on Kerberos and ready Beahl's crew for their assignments. As his favored strategist, I'll have to guide and instruct on every weapon and its placement. This is actually a blessing because tomorrow, we can avoid them all with ease. I'll know where each merc hides, where every guard lurks, and the weapons they will have at their disposal. Our plan is a thing of beauty.

At some point this afternoon, I have to meet Bruce outside the commons to set up our diversion and clear the bridge. Bruce will sneak in and disarm the implant remote, and no one, including Beahl, will be the wiser. At least, not until he tries to use it. Even then, unless we're in his line of sight, he won't have a clue that the device isn't working.

I sneak into the hall and creep silently to Aine's cell. I am light on feet despite my size. My training has turned me into a predator, and if I don't wish to be seen or heard, I'm not. When I reach her cell, my breath hitches in my chest, and I feel my mate's hearts tug at my own. She is still asleep, ethereal with her lips slightly parted, and I watch the gentle rise and fall of her breasts as she slumbers. My body aches to go to her, to hold her, to claim her.

"Griz?"

A sleepy voice breaks through the silence, surprising me. I've made no sound at all, cast no shadow, yet, my mate still felt my presence. This pleases me greatly.

"Good morning, amavi. You are well?"

She slides out of her bed, rubbing her eyes as her little feet pad toward me. Gods, she is so beautiful.

"I'm well, but I missed you."

Her words turn my hard, warrior's heart to jelly. "Come to me, sweetling."

I wrap her warm soft body in my arms and pull her close to my chest. Then, I kiss and nuzzle her neck, nipping at her ear until I feel her shiver. "You know that you are mine, don't you?"

"Yes."

Her warm breath puffs against her mark on my neck, and her submission drives a bolt of lust straight to my cock.

"Soon, we will be together, amavi, and I will never leave your bed."

She is quiet for a moment as I cuddle her, softly stroking her back. Then, the fragrant bouquet of her arousal assails me. My fangs extend, and a feral growl erupts from my chest as I tighten my grip, crushing her to me.

"Why are you growling at me?"

I rest my forehead against hers and smile at the depth of her innocence. "Because you want me, sweetling. Your body is ready to be claimed by its mate."

She pauses for a moment, her eyes glistening as she trails her little finger across my chest. "So, do it, then."

My brain sputters. My cock feels like a one-ton hammer in my pants, and my balls are so tight, I think they've totally disappeared. My pants are damp with pre-cum, and my hand is already reaching for my drawstring before I can even catch myself.

"Goddess help me, Aine. I can't. Not here. Not now," I

pant.

"But I need you, Griz," she tells me, her voice husky with desire as her fingers trail across my nipples.

Godsdammit. I'm not sure if I'm going to survive this. I try to control my breathing, but I think I may be hyperventilating. Has that ever happened to a Tarilean warrior before?

I drop to my knees, grazing my face down the satiny fabric of her gown, until my nose is pressed hard against her pussy. I grab a breast firmly in each hand, pinching her nipples as I inhale deeply. Gods, she smells divine. With her gasps, I nearly pass out from the need to claim her.

"Griz," she whimpers, driving her hands into my hair and tugging my face toward her core.

With one last pinch of her nipples, I drag my hands down the front of her gown, lifting it and burying my head beneath. I place my hands on her thighs, roughly spreading her legs and forcing her feet apart. Then, I part her pretty, pink folds with my fingers and plunge my tongue inside her.

Keening, she thrusts her hips forward and claws at the hem of her gown. Then, her fingers are in my hair again, twisting and pulling my face harder to her.

"Oh, god, Griz," she pants.

Frizzuck! My control is in shreds, and I feel myself sinking into the mating frenzy as my mate's sweet juices slide past my tongue and down my throat. I could sip her forever, but I have to keep it together. My mate needs relief. She needs me.

Slowly, I withdraw my tongue and glide it through her silky folds. I leave no part of her untouched as I move to gently circle her clit. Her breath hitches and she moans, rocking her hips against me impatiently. It's time to give my mate the relief she needs. Slowly, I press my finger inside her, careful of her maidenhead as I swish my tongue across her clit. Then, I feel her tight channel begin to flutter. I close my lips around her, nipping lightly as I suck.

"Griz!"

I hold her up as her knees buckle and her body clenches around my finger over and over. Holy frizzuck! My cock explodes in my pants again, jerking and releasing my seed with every spasm of her channel. I let the orgasm flow through me as I lick her softly through the aftershocks. Then, I peer up at her lovely face, gentle in her bliss. She takes my breath away.

Her half-lidded eyes gaze down at me, and she smiles. "That was wonderful."

I heartily agree.

I make sure she's solid on her feet before I stand up, trying to hide the large wet stain across the entire front of my pants. "Sweetling, I will bring you pleasure every day for the rest of our lives. That is just a small taste of what awaits you."

Her face pinkens, and it's all I can do not to try and tear down the bars that separate us.

"My amavi is so beautiful."

She places her soft hand on my cheek and rises to her tiptoes to kiss me.

"So are you," she whispers.

I grab her wrist in my hand, planting a gentle kiss to her palm before pressing it against my chest. "I have to go now, meishkala. There is much to be done before tomorrow. You must be ready to leave at any time once we land on Kerberos."

She nods vigorously. "We will be."

Huh?

"We?"

"Yes," she replies, scrunching her cute little nose. "We. Me and the girls."

"What girls?"

She stares at me incredulously.

"Those girls," she says, waving her arm in the direction of the other cells.

My hearts start beating out of rhythm with each other, and

my chest begins to cramp. I know I need to handle this most delicately. "Amavi, dearest. We cannot take them with us. Not tomorrow."

"What?"

Her eyes glisten, and for a moment, I fear they may start leaking again. They don't, thank the goddess. Instead, they fill with fire, and her anger becomes a blazing wall between us.

"I'm not leaving them here, Griz. I won't go without them."

"Then, none of us will make it out of here. There's no way. I promise we will send help as soon as we're free."

"No," she insists, her cute little chin tilting in the same stubborn defiance as her sire. "If they don't go, neither do I. And, frankly, I can't believe that you would just leave them here."

Godsdammit. It's so hard to deny my mate anything. It's like sandpaper against my soul to tell her no, but I have to get her to safety. I cannot protect her here, and there's no way I can get them all out. I will have to be strong and hope that she forgives me soon.

"Aine. You're not being reasonable. You must trust that I know what's best for you when I tell you that you're going with me tomorrow. Now, let that be the end of it."

Apparently, that isn't the right thing to say to an angry mate. How am I supposed to know?

The promise of swift death swirls in her luminesce eyes, and she speaks to me through gritted teeth.

"No. I. Will. Not. And, *that's* the end of it. Take Bruce with you. I'll be going with the girls after we take down the guards and steal their weapons and keys. Now, which way are the escape pods in case we don't get out fast enough to make land?"

Taking down guards? Stealing weapons? Flying escape pods? "Eh . . . Uh . . . Er . . ."

I know I'm making words. There are millions of those little

word things floating around in my head right now, crawling over each other to get out. But, for some reason, they seem to be stuck in my throat.

"Over my dead body!"

Of all those great little words I had lined up, those are the ones that finally come spilling out. My mate's eyes turn all squinty like Bruce's and then become hard as steel.

"Keep out of my way, alien," she growls, and I flinch in shock.

My mate growled! At me!

"Aine—" I plan to try pleading with her next, but she cuts me off, throwing her palm in the air and stifling me with a deadly glare.

"The subject is closed. We are through discussing. Now, which way are the pods?"

I point a shaky finger toward the escape exits, baffled, and trying to figure out how to put an end to this madness.

"Near the engine rooms," I vaguely hear myself saying.

"Thank you. You better go now and get started on all those things you have to get done by tomorrow. If I don't see you before, then I'll see you and Bruce on Kerberos."

What in the Haelic is this crazy female saying?

"Goodbye, Griz," she says, effectively dismissing me as she spins on her heel and strides back across the cell to her cot.

Good goddess. I'm late, and now, I have to talk to Bruce before I can do anything else. I stalk back through the cells, to Haelic with stealth now, and nearly burst into flames beneath the burning gazes of at least a hundred unified femkis from across the universe. By the time I make it through the exit, I feel like I've just been to war with Goridians.

I hurry, speeding through the corridors, pushing servants and bots aside, jumping over food carts and laundry trolleys until I finally reach Bruce's door. I pound on it until he answers, ignoring his floppy cock as I brush past him.

"She won't come!" I shout like a lunatic.

"Quiet, lad," he chides, scratching his bare ass as he steps out in the hall to look for witnesses. I pace back and forth until he steps back inside and closes the door behind him. "Now, what do you mean she won't come? She—"

He stops mid-sentence and glares at the wet spot around my crotch. "What the holy feck is that on your pants?"

Shiest! I grab a pillow off his bed and shove it front of me.

"Not my feckin' pillow, you numpty!"

He leaps at me, snatching it out of my hand and tossing it back on his bed.

I growl at him, frustrated and ready to snap. *Foolish human.*

"Now, when you say my daughter won't come, I ken you weren't meaning—" he drops his eyes to the big stain on the front of my pants.

"What?" I shout. "Gods, no. Not, she won't *come*." I pause at the thought, my cock suddenly taking a keen interest in the conversation. She came, all right. I shake my head to clear it and then continue. "I mean she won't come with us tomorrow. She says she won't leave without the other femkis."

"That's impossible," he huffs.

"I told her that! She says they have some crazy plan to attack the guards, steal their weapons, and then escape through the emergency pod exits."

"That's just fecking crazy," he shouts at me.

"I know! I told her that! What should I do?"

I look at him expectantly, and he stares back, his face a question mark.

"How the feck should I know?" he finally replies.

"You're her sire. She needs to be disciplined."

"Well, you're her big, bad fated husband or some such havering. You discipline her."

We stare blankly at each other for a few silent moments, and then both collapse into the chairs.

"You tried talking to her, you say?"

"Yes, of course. She would not listen to reason. What do you normally do when she won't listen?"

He scratches his head. "Hell, I don't rightly ken. She's usually the one talking reason to me."

*Useless human.* We fall back into silence.

"Spank her," he finally says. "You're going to have to spank her. I've never disciplined her before. That's her problem. But I ain't seen a woman yet who didn't need a good spanking every now and then, and it's actually quite . . . um . . . cathartic for both parties." His face takes on a distant, nostalgic quality, and when he speaks again, his voice has dropped a full octave, turning all hoarse and gravelly. It's then that I notice he's still naked. "Why, I remember this one time, her mum and I —"

"Stop!" I throw my palm at him, like Aine did to me while ago. Floppy cock Bruce is bad enough. I can't risk excited Bruce. "I cannot spank her for disciplinary purposes. I have not yet claimed her."

"That's pretty obvious," he says, rolling his eyes at my crotch.

"We'll just have to change our plan," I tell him, ignoring his last remark.

"Our plan is perfect the way it is! We'll never come up with another one before tomorrow."

I sigh. "Get dressed. I have an idea."

# CHAPTER FOURTEEN

Aine

After collapsing back on my foul, smelly cot, my whole body quakes with anger. How could they possibly think I would leave all those poor, defenseless women behind? Do I really seem like that kind of person? The kind of person concerned only about saving her own ass?

Maybe Griz thinks I'm that selfish. No matter how I feel about him, we've technically only known each other for a couple of days. But Bruce? Did Bruce actually think I would opt to save myself and damn the consequences? Not a chance in Hell I could do something like that. I'd never forgive myself.

I glance toward the hall and breathe a sigh of relief. Thank goodness he left. I was afraid for a moment that he would just stand there and stare at me all morning with those damn puppy dog eyes of his. I sigh and flip over on my side. Angry as I am, I can't help but think about what we did this morning. What *he* did.

I feel myself growing wet again as I remember the way his rough hands laid open my thighs, the smooth glide of his fingers along my girlie bits, and not least of all, his wicked tongue as he swiped it back and forth across my clit. My pussy flutters in response, and I squeeze my thighs together. As expected, it offers no relief. I need Griz.

Just stop! I'm pissed at him right now. I don't care how talented his appendages are, he can't just boss me around like that. "Me know best. You come with Griz. End of story," he

104

says like some freaking barbarian. Like he's lord and master over my body.

*He is.*

No, dammit, he's not.

I growl realizing I've now been reduced to having full-blown arguments with myself. This is ridiculous. I have to focus on getting us out of here since, obviously, Griz and Bruce aren't going to help. I roll off my cot and creep back toward the bars. ES Four Three Nine will be along shortly with breakfast, and I may not have another chance to talk to the girls for a while.

"Psst," I hiss. "Celia? Jill? Are you awake?"

"Aine, the entire cell block is awake after your boyfriend's little conjugal visit. Like anyone could have slept through that," Celia replies.

Suddenly, I'm glad we're separated by thick concrete-like walls and that they can't see me blushing violently from head to toe.

"They do have escape pods. They're by the engineering room," I tell her, ignoring her comment.

"Great! Did he happen to tell you where Engineering was?"

"He told me what direction to go," I reply defensively.

"Aine, I still don't get how you can understand him. He talks in gibberish just like the rest of them," Jill says.

Shoot. I meant to ask Griz about that this morning. For some reason, my brain turns to mush whenever he's around. "I don't know, Jill. I just do."

"If you can speak their language, can't you just tell these other girls about our plan? Why are Jill and I having to play alien charades?"

"I can't really speak their language. Somehow, I just understand the words when they speak them. It's hard to explain."

Clanging keys signal the arrival of breakfast, and I wait to hear the now familiar sound of ES Four Three Nine making her rounds. But that's not the sound that follows.

"Back there," a deep, harsh voice says. "All the way to the very back."

Oh, shit. That's me. I'm the one in the very back. I slink into the corner, trying to make myself as small a target as possible. Within a few seconds, several of the scaly, lizard guys are standing in front of my cell holding a big, metal tub full of steaming water. At least, I think it's water. Are they going to cook me?

These guys are different from the usual guards. They're larger and look more like disciplined soldiers than hired thugs. I've never seen them before. What the hell is going on?

They step aside, making room for a tall, creepy lizard-man in a blue velvet waistcoat who approaches with a key in his hand. He gives me a cocksure smile as he puts the key in the lock and turns it. A subsequent "clink" tells me that this guy has the key that fits. This must be Beahl.

Swathed in confidence, he radiates authority. Bright red scales peek out from beneath the neckline of his coat, making his chest appear to glow. There are swirly gold emblems on his jacket sleeves, and his pants are black, not green like the other guys. No, he's not like the others, and even though he doesn't appear to be armed, I can tell he's much more danger- ous. This one is definitely the boss.

The door swings open, and he steps aside to let the others in. "Put it over there next to the bed."

I watch with a morbid curiosity as they sidle the tub next to my cot. When they've finished, they stand there ramrod straight, never once glancing in my direction. Instead, they look expectantly at the lizard man in the blue waistcoat.

"That'll be all. You can go," he says.

The largest one gives him a dubious look, obviously un- comfortable with the directive. "Pardon me, sir. But, perhaps we should wait over by the exit?"

"Why would you do that? Do I look like I'm in danger here?" he asks with a mocking tone. "Do I look like I might be overwhelmed by that tiny female?"

He points at me, and for the first time since they arrived, they all turn their heads to study me.

"Of course not, sir. My apologies," the guy finally answers. Then, he turns to face the others. "Move out."

Blue Waistcoat Guy saunters over to my cot and drops a small bag onto the middle of it while the others filter out. I watch as the last one steps through, leaving the cell door ajar behind him. My brain has a quick argument with my feet. One says run like hell, and the other says not to bother. Apparently, Blue Waistcoat Guy picks up on my internal struggle, because he laughs.

"You could try, but you wouldn't get very far." He chuckles. "Come here, female."

My eyes drop to his belt first thing, furiously searching for a welter whip. He's not wearing one, but I sense he doesn't really need one to hurt me.

"I can see you're going to need some basic training before we get to Janyx." He sighs. "Although, the thought of punishing you does sound appealing. I said, come here."

My legs feel like spaghetti, and I'm not sure I could move even if I wanted to, which I don't. My eyes dart around the room in a panic, searching for something, anything.

"I know you understand me, female. You have five clicks to come to me, or I'll come to you. You don't want that to happen because I'll probably be angry by the time I get there."

What's that famous Helen Keller quote? *Never bend your head. Always hold it high and look the world straight in the eye.* Easy for her to say. She was blind, and not about to be raped by a giant lizard.

I can do this. Standing straight, I dig deep for some of that courage I know is buried in me somewhere. Then, I square my shoulders and tip my chin defiantly. Taking a deep breath,

I look him straight in his beady eyes and walk slowly toward him, leaving only a few paces between us.

"That's better," he says, studying me with piercing scrutiny. "But, the next time you hesitate when I give an order, you'll be punished. Do you know who I am?"

Spawn of Hitler? Satan? The Phantom of the Opera? "Beahl?"

"That's right. You may call me Master," he says. "Or, sir."

Like hell.

"Now, did you tell one of my bots that you needed to bathe?"

Dammit. I did. My calculated risk not only didn't pay off, it appears to have backfired in a major way. I blink at him, trying to decide the best response.

He begins circling me, pausing behind me, and before I have a chance to answer his question, I feel his cold fingers at the nape of my neck. Then, suddenly, my dress floats down my body and pools in a silky puddle around my ankles. I suck in a deep breath as the cold air sinks into my skin, causing my nipples to harden and goosebumps to swim up and down my arms. In a reflexive response, I throw my arms across my breasts and squeeze my legs together.

He walks slowly around to face me, his eyes cold and hard as I hold his gaze defiantly. Then, like a snake striking, he lashes out and wraps his long fingers around my neck, squeezing painfully. I grasp and claw at his arms, my nails not even making a dent in his scales. His eyes glisten with excitement, and it's obvious how much he likes this. The bastard's getting off on it.

"Hands at your sides, female."

I let the swell of anger and hatred radiate through me as my hands drift back down to my sides. He smirks, loosening his grip on my neck as his eyes wander down to my breasts, and then lower.

"Good. You're learning. Mm," he says, as if he's performing some kind of medical inspection. "We'll need to remove this."

Reaching down, he tugs at my pubic hair.

It shocks the crap out of me, and I cry out, jumping back out of his reach. His eyes narrow threateningly in a look that promises pain, so I take a step forward in hopes of fending off whatever attack he's contemplating. It seems to work, and instead of striking out again, he continues his methodic inspection until he's standing behind me again, his chest against my back.

"You're quite an attractive specimen," he whispers in my ear. "Maybe I'll train you myself."

I say nothing. I'm afraid if I open my mouth, there's no telling what might come out.

His cold fingers wrap like a vise around my wrists, and he jerks them behind me painfully, holding them in one hand while his other grips the back of my neck. Pushing against my arms, he forces me to lean forward.

"That's it. Bend over," he says. "Now, spread your legs."

The fuck you say? I'm not about to spread anything. I press my legs together tighter. Suddenly, I hear a loud crack, and then, a fierce lick of fire burns across my bare ass.

"I said, spread!" he growls.

Cursing under my breath, I wiggle my feet a tiny bit apart. Not satisfied, he slides his boot between my legs and nudges them even further until I'm damn near bent over and doing the splits. I've never felt so exposed in my life. Leaning over, he runs a long, bony finger through my dry folds and begins to toggle my clit.

I shriek, my body tensing but unable to straighten up with my arms twisted behind my back.

"Ah. A pleasure button," he muses. "And, such a unique scent."

He glides his finger back through my folds and nudges at my asshole. I tense again and stiffen, trying to wriggle away in spite of the pain in my arms. It gets me nothing except another brutal slap to my ass.

Gasping, I can't stop the tears that swell in my eyes.

"Now, stand still," he says as he continues his prodding. "What about this back hole? Have you ever had a cock in here?"

I feel my face flush, shame and embarrassment washing through me like a dirty tide. "No!"

Smack! Another assault on my ass, even harder than the first two, pushes out a few tears this time.

"No what?"

Confused, it takes a moment to figure out what he wants. When, I do, I see red.

"No, *sir*," I grit, and he continues on with his inspection as if he hadn't been interrupted.

"Hm. I wonder if it will decrease your value if I take your back hole? I'll have to ask Ceazare," he muses as he swipes his finger back and forth over it.

I swoon and a swell of nausea nearly claims me. Finally, he releases me, and I can straighten again, my arms aching as I try to rub them back to life.

"You never answered my question," he says as he steps in front of me again, reaching out to casually tweak my nipple.

I flinch, but don't move from my spot. "What question?"

"I'm not used to repeating myself. I don't like it," he warns. "Did you or did you not ask to bathe?"

*Fork-chop!* I glance at my cot and see the end of it sticking out from beneath the blanket beside the bag he dropped.

"I did," I reply.

"Well, here you are, then. A bath." He chuckles as he waves a hand behind him at the tub. "Let it not be said that you don't have a generous master. Now, get in so I can wash you."

I'm a second away from pouncing on the fork-chop when the door at the end of the hall opens. *Please, God. Don't let it be Griz.*

"Sir!" A gruff, masculine voice rings out from down the hall. "We have a situation."

"Froecking idiots," he mumbles and rolls his eyes as if we're sharing an inside joke. Then, he reaches out and grabs my wrist, pulling me toward the tub. "Well, handle it! I'm busy," he shouts back.

"We've got two missing crew, sir. Shan and Balda. Neither showed up for duty, and they haven't been sighted since last night."

*Griz!* I barely manage to swallow my excitement, focusing to keep my face blank. Blue Waistcoat Guy's eye twitches, and he snarls as he releases me.

"I'll be right there," he shouts.

When the sound of the big door clanging shut echoes down the hallway, he turns glazed eyes to mine and grasps my hand in his. "Sorry for the interruption, pet. We'll have plenty of time to get to know one another before we get to Janyx, though. There's soap and a clean sarka in that bag on the bed. Get cleaned up, and I'll come back later, after I take care of this. I'll try to talk to Ceasare about your back hole, too."

My stomach roils. The way he says it, as if I should be sad he's leaving or looking forward to his return so he can plunder my ass, makes me wonder if he's a pancake short of a full stack.

He strides out of the cell, clicking the door shut and locking it behind him. When I'm sure he's gone and I've heard the door at the end of the hall boom shut once again, I grab the soap and washcloth and do my best to scrub him off my skin. Then, I step into the clean dress he left and slide it up my body, clasping it behind my neck. When I'm done, I take slow, measured steps over to my toilet, and I lean over and vomit.

# CHAPTER FIFTEEN

Griz

"There!" I huff, stepping back to assess my work.

I've propped Shan's cold, lifeless body next to his headless friend's and arranged them both in one of the darker, less traveled sections in the aft of the ship. I reach out and tip his head slightly so that it's leaning against Balda's shoulder, and then, I place Balda's severed head in Shan's lap.

"I'm starting to wonder about you, alien," Bruce says as he eyes the macabre display in front of us.

"What? Do you think I'm enjoying this?" I snap. "At least, I didn't put his cock in Shan's mouth. Now, get his blaster and his keys while I get Shan's."

I jerk my head toward Balda as I stuff my hand in Shan's pocket and fish around for the keys or anything else that might help us.

"I still don't ken why you didn't just take this stuff right when you killed them," he grumbles, tentatively sliding his hand inside Balda's jacket. He leans his upper body back as far as he can, determined not to get too close.

"Why would I have done that? I can't take over the entire ship with a couple of little blasters and a few keys. Besides, none of these work on Aine's cell."

"But, you're sure they'll open the other ones?" Slowly, he pulls a ring of keys from Balda's inside pocket.

"Yes. I'm sure," I tell him, hoping it's true.

"What's this?" he asks, now holding a torsion wrench in

the air as he studies it.

Hallelujah! "It's the key to Aine's cell!" I laugh.

"This thing?"

I snatch it from him and fist it in my hand. If we can't get the key from Beahl, this is the next best thing. With this, we can get her out. We can save them all.

The look on Aine's face when she told me of the guards' assault on the other femkis the night before still haunts me. It was enough to condemn my conscience and shake me from my complacency.

A stark, horrifying realization hits me. She's right. Aine is right. I should have done something a long time ago. I should never have sat back idly and let them suffer at the hands of these fiends as I did. Even if it meant dying in the process, I should have acted, done something. Maybe my dam would have gone free if there was no longer a need to control me. Or, if Beahl was dead.

By the Goddess, I have no idea what is right or wrong anymore. Save them and condemn my dam? Save my dam and sacrifice the lives of all these femkis? I feel like my soul is being torn in two.

I had let them strip me of my own sense of duty and rightness with every fresh assault on my dignity, and had let my pride keep me from fighting for their freedom. I had grown more apathetic with each new humiliation until I didn't care about anything or anyone except myself.

"You look like you just swallowed a dirty arsehole. What's wrong with you?"

Bruce's words wake me from my reverie. My head hung and my shoulders drooping, I shake my head.

"It can't be that bad," he says. "I didn't really mean what I said before. I ken you're a good fella."

"It's not that." My voice cracks, and I feel the words rip at my throat as I spit them out. "I cannot claim Aine. She deserves more. I have no honor. They've stolen it, along with my freedom and my conscience. I would only bring her shame."

Bruce stands up, his head swiveling up and down the hallway nervously. "Uh . . . look here, lad. Now's not really the best time to get into this."

I stand up, take a deep breath and nod as I slip Shan's blaster and keys into my pocket. "I know. Let's go."

I turn to make my way back toward the emergency coms, but Bruce grabs my arm and spins me around.

"You ain't lost nothing you can't get back. I don't ken what you did or you think you did, but take it from me, someone who kens a thing or two about lost honor. It ain't never too late to do the right thing."

His eyes sparkle with a deep, hidden wisdom I've not seen from him before, and I begin to wonder if there's more to this little human than meets the eye. Either way, his words fill me with renewed determination, and I think maybe all is not lost, after all. Maybe it's really not too late to redeem myself.

"Can you find the bridge all right once I set off the emergency alarm?"

"Is a Scotsman naked beneath his kilt?"

I curl my lip at his crazy talk and wonder how I could have mistaken him for wise just a few clicks ago.

Releasing my arm, he huffs with exasperation and produces a single key from his pocket. "Aye. I can find the bridge. And here's the key I found in that fella Beahl's desk drawer. It's the only one that was there. I thought it was the key that opened Aine's cell, but if you already found it on that dead guy—"

I snatch it greedily from his hand, not even angry that he didn't tell me sooner, and give him an enthusiastic pat on the arm that sends him reeling into the wall beside us.

"Easy there, laddie. We're on the same side, remember?"

He rubs his arm and gives me an annoyed look.

"I'll take the keys to Aine while you deactivate the remote. Be very sure everyone's off the bridge before you go in."

"I ken. I've got this. Just do your own job." He draws his furry brows together and glares at me.

My lips quirk into a smile, amused by his fierceness. I can't resist annoying him further by repeating our plan for the tenth time since we started out. "And, remember, if you get in there and find you can't deactivate it, just leave. Get out of there before they get back. We'll find another way."

"I ken what I'm doing, alien!" He snarls at me, his face beginning to tic. "Dinnae teach yer Granny tae suck eggs!"

I have no idea what he's talking about, but his face is turning red and his eye keeps twitching. I chuckle as he takes off in a jog down the hall.

"Bruce!"

He stops and spins around, no doubt ready to take a swing at me.

"What?" he snaps.

"It's that way," I tell him, pointing in the other direction.

With alarms blaring and blue lights blinking on and off all around me, I slip back into the holding area again. I have to hurry this time. As soon as they find Shan and Balda, security will be on high alert, and patrols will be doubled. I race through the long line of cells, acutely feeling the confused, questioning gazes of the femkis as I pass by. Ignoring their inquiries, I make a dive toward the bars of Aine's cell and nearly crumble when I find her retching over her toilet.

"Aine!"

She throws her hand up behind her, shifting her feet so I can't see her face as she heaves again.

"Amavi, are you ill?"

She stands up slowly, raking her forearm across her mouth

and taking a deep breath before she turns to look at me. Her face is flushed and taut, and my only thought is to comfort her.

I hold out my arms, praying that she will come to me. I don't care what she said this morning. I don't care that we quarreled or that I'm not worthy of her bravery or her kindness. I just need to comfort my mate. After a moment of hesitation, she rushes to me, and I crush her to my chest. She needs this. I need this.

Plying her hair with kisses, I close my eyes and rock her against me. "It's okay, my little princess. Everything will be okay."

"Griz," she sobs. "I'm sorry."

I chuckle. "There is nothing to be sorry for, sweetling. You were right. We will all leave this place together."

She says nothing else for a moment and then cocks her head, listening to the alarms as if she's only just now heard them. "What is that horrible noise? And, why are all the lights blinking like that?"

I chuckle. "Your sire and I created a diversion."

"What kind of diversion? For what?"

"Bruce is taking care of a problem for us. I'll explain later." I squeeze her tighter in my arms and lay my cheek atop her head. Then, I notice the huge tub of water sitting beside her bed.

"What is that, amavi?" I ask, releasing her and holding her at arm's length so I can look at her face.

She scrubs both hands over her cheeks, roughly wiping her tears, and then scowls at the tub. "A bath."

"I see," I tell her, but not really seeing anything at all. "The bath made you ill?"

She laughs, but it is hollow and empty. "No, the bath didn't make me ill. The creep who came with it did."

I feel the blood draining from my face. I don't have to ask

her who or what. There's only one male with a key to her cell, besides me now, and she's freshly bathed and wearing a clean beshaba. I know what happened.

"Did he . . . harm you?" I wait for her answer, my stomach clenching, but she says nothing. My pulse beats faster with every click, and my hearts break for my mate. "I'll kill him."

"No. He didn't hurt me. He didn't have time," she finally says. "Your . . . *diversion* saved me."

"Amavi," I whisper, pressing my lips to her cheek. Thank the Goddess.

She brushes her hands across my chest. "He only hurt my pride. This time. But he'll be back."

I don't ask her anything else about it. I don't want to know what he did to her, if he touched her, defiled her in any way. I don't think I can bear it. I am not as strong as my mate, and I can't afford to alter our plans by killing Beahl immediately.

I take the blaster and a set of keys from my pocket and push them through the bars to her. "Take these."

She gasps. "Griz! How?"

I say nothing, but she gleans understanding.

"Shan." She smirks.

"And, this one," I say, removing a large silver key from my other pocket and handing it to her. "This one opens your cell."

I smile as she takes the key, her mouth falling open as she stares in disbelief.

"Griz, how did you get this?"

"I didn't. I was going to try to blasting you out or picking the lock. You can thank Bruce later."

"Bruce? You've got to be kidding me."

I chuckle, fisting my hand around hers as she clenches her freedom in the palm of her hand. "Hide them all beneath your bed until we set down on Kerberos. Don't come out until you feel the engines power down, and the gravity starts to change."

She nods, her expression serious and her attention firmly anchored on me. I give her a reassuring smile, hoping it's enough to recharge her resolution.

"It's important to wait until you're sure we've set down before you release the other femkis. Do you understand?"

"Yes. I understand." She nods.

"Once you free them, don't make a sound. Wait by the door until Bruce arrives. He will lead you to the exit."

"What about the guards?"

I lean forward and give my brave, precious mate a kiss on her forehead. "Let me worry about them. But, if you do run into anyone, you mustn't hesitate. Do whatever you have to, but get to the exit. You and Bruce are both armed. This will be our only chance, mate."

A flash of fear flickers in her eyes, but it's gone almost instantly, replaced with a quiet, determined courage.

"We'll make it out," she says sternly.

"Are you afraid, my little warrior?"

"No. Yes," she admits reluctantly. "But, I can handle it. At least, I get to fight, and that's a helluva lot better than sitting in here feeling helpless and afraid."

"Let's hope you don't have to fight too much," I tell her, my guts wringing at the thought of my mate in a fire fight. "Just stay close to Bruce. You'll have a better chance if you run into trouble, and I'll come to you as soon as I can."

When she smiles at me, I feel sure that this morning's harsh words are all but forgotten, and the terrible weight of her unhappiness melts from my shoulders. I can finally breathe again.

Once I've shown her how to operate the blaster, I give her a few quick tips on how and where to aim in the event she runs into any resistance. Then, I instruct her on navigating the ship's curvy, convoluted corridors. I've memorized every twist and turn from here to the starboard exit, and now, I make her recite them back to me.

"Left, right, right, left, left, right, left, left," she says for the third time, and I nod proudly.

"That's it. Just don't panic, and keep everyone quiet until you exit the ship."

I'd feel much better if I could be with her tomorrow, but I have to lead the raiding party. I've arranged for almost half the crew to be with me outside the ship. If I suggest any more than that, Beahl will get suspicious. It's all I can do, but it just doesn't feel like enough. Still, my mate exudes the calm and confidence of an experienced Tarilean warrior, and I could not be any prouder.

After kissing her thoroughly, I slip back out of the holding area and hurry toward my room. It's all I can do not to go and find Bruce, to make sure he got the remote deactivated successfully. I'll just have to trust that all went according to plan. I will be the first person Beahl suspects when they find Shan and Balda, and I need to be safe in my quarters when he turns his eyes to me. I can't risk missing tomorrow's raid. Everything depends on it. I've no choice but to lay low until I meet up with Bruce in the morning.

Finally, my door in sight, I breathe out a sigh of relief. I can hardly believe my good fortune. I didn't run into a single soul on my way back. It was almost too easy. Goddess knows, it's about frizzucking time the fates swung some good luck my way.

With no lock on the flimsy door of my apartment, I waste no time hurrying inside. I flip on the lights as soon as I enter and manage one step into the living area before I curse the fates again.

"Griz! I'm glad you could finally join us," Beahl purrs from his relaxed position on my sofa. "Look guys. Griz is back."

As I stand there wondering how the ten black ops mercs in my front room could all fit inside my tiny living room, I don't even notice the eleventh one who slips up behind me. I barely even feel it when he clubs me over the head with the butt of his blaster, or when unconsciousness begins to darken the corners of my eyes.

But, my last thought I feel with acute clarity and with every beat of my hearts.

*Aine.*

# CHAPTER SIXTEEN

Aine

"Psst. Aine. You there?"
Jill's small voice floats down the hall to me, and I run to the bars.

"I'm here," I reply, still trying to float back to the ground after Griz's amazing kiss.

"Duh. Where else would she be?" Celia quips.

I almost make a snarky reply, but then, she does something unheard of. She actually says something nice.

"Listen, Aine. We don't really know what happened earlier . . . with that lizard bastard, I mean. Don't want to know. But, don't let the assholes get to you. Here's a little trick I learned back home. Just close your eyes and go somewhere else, let your mind take you somewhere they can't reach, and stay there until the fuckers leave. It works. Believe me, in my line of work, I've used this technique plenty."

In her line of work?

"And, remember, they can take our bodies, but they can't take our souls," she says. "Or, our hearts and minds. They can't touch those."

"I know. I'm fine," I tell her, and, to my surprise, I find I really am. Through focusing, I've turned the whole ordeal into anger, instead, and it's only making me more determined.

"Thank you, Celia. Is everyone set to go?"

"Not unless the guards come back tonight. We still don't

have a key," Jill says.

I smile and jingle the keys that Griz brought me through the bars. The girls gasp, and I feel their excitement charging the air.

"What is that?" Celia asks hopefully.

"You got them? She got them!" Jill all but giggles.

"Shh," It's my turn to chide. "Griz says we'll set down in the morning, before dawn. We need to make sure we're awake and ready to go."

"No problem. I doubt I'll even close my eyes tonight," Jill says with a sigh.

"Well, that won't be a problem for me. I've been too wound up to sleep for days now. Wake me up when we get there," Celia replies.

I managed to nap on and off throughout the night, though plagued with strange, lucid dreams that felt so real, I woke up punching at the empty air in front of me. I was terrified that we'd land, and I would somehow manage to sleep through it. Without a window, it seemed quite possible. Finally, giving up on sleep, I pace back and forth in my cell, instead. Too much nervous energy.

I've barely made it two full laps when the floor begins to shake and shimmy beneath my feet. Before my teeth even stop rattling, it ends as abruptly as it started. The air around me suddenly grows denser, thicker, and my limbs feel bulky, like they're weighed down. It's nothing that prevents me from moving. More like I've just eaten two full-course Thanksgiving dinners back to back, with a whole pie for dessert.

Is this it? Are we on Kerberos?

The ship releases one last shudder followed by a loud metallic belch. Then, there's nothing. I stand there for a couple of uncertain moments before lunging beneath my cot for the blaster and the keys. I have to hold the key to my cell at a weird angle to hit the lock, and my hands tremble like I have a nervous detox condition. I almost drop the stupid thing twice. Finally, I feel it sink home, and when I give it a little twist, the bulky tumblers click into place, and the door pops ajar.

With a relieved sigh, I push it open and jog over to the next cell. Nothing—not seven-feet-tall barbarians, goggly-eyed robots, scaly lizard men, or even giant talking frogs—has prepared me for what I see when I get there.

"I told you," says the curvy young blonde standing in front me. She props her hands on her hips and turns to the little brunette beside her, bobbing her head and pointing at me. "She's wigging out. I knew she didn't believe me."

I may not recognize the face, but I'd know that voice anywhere. "Celia!"

She turns her attention back to me, not missing a beat. "Alien. Freaks. I knew you didn't believe me when I told you what we were dealing with over here."

I glance around at the throng of other prisoners, almost not believing my eyes. Most are obviously feminine, but some are . . . well, they're just not. Or, rather, it's hard to tell. There are tall blue ones, short red ones, medium green ones. There's even a few purple ones peppered throughout the odd crowd. Some have pincers in place of hands, some have long tentacles instead of arms, and some even have more than one set of arms.

The one thing they all seem to have in common is a strong desire to get the hell out of here. They start pressing toward the bars impatiently, grunting and growling at each another, and the commotion begins to stir the prisoners in the other cells.

"Shh. Quiet!" I glare at them, at the same time hoping that my finger against my lips is a universally known signal for shut the fuck up. It must be, because they begin to settle.

"Well, don't just stand there gawking. Get us the hell out of here!" Celia says with her face squished up against the bars.

I give myself a firm mental slap and lift the messy wad of keys on the huge ring. Squinting in the dim light, I begin stabbing each one into the door frantically.

"I'm Jill, by the way," the brunette says even as she's being smashed into the bars.

Smiling, I glance up from my task to formally introduce myself, and I'm caught short by the nasty bruises on her face. Those bastards. My disgust must be obvious, because she looks away and sighs.

"I know. I think it must look worse than it really is."

Embarrassed by my reaction, I don't respond to her comment. Instead, I focus my attention back on the lock and keys. "It's just nice to finally have a face to go with the voice."

"Same here," Jill says as she watches me struggle with the keys.

Every one of them I try fails, and I'm starting to sweat bullets. What if none of these fits?

"Hang on, ladies. It's got to be one of these," I say, trying more to convince myself than them.

With only a few untried keys left, I take another stab, and the key melts into the lock. A quick flick of my wrist, and the door springs open. Without pausing, I move on to the next cell, which is even more crowded than Jill's and Celia's. It takes no time at all, though, now that I've found the right key, and I breeze through it. Each clinking lock is like music to my ears, and then, I'm off to the next one. I do this four times, finding that the other cells have twice as many girls in them as Jill's and Celia's. There has to be at least a hundred females in here.

By the time I make it to the end, the occupants are becoming restless and desperate. They dart around all over the place, shoving me out of the way, and clawing at each other to get to the exit.

"No! Wait!" I try to shout without actually yelling, but it doesn't do any good. No one is paying a damn bit of attention to me, except maybe Jill and Celia. The crazy females are starting to get loud, fighting each other to get to the door first. "Stop! We have to wait."

I may as well be farting the national anthem with all the good it does. No one listens. The large door at the front of the room groans open, and the hall is suddenly bathed in light from the corridor outside. I watch in horror as at least one hundred frantic, alien females start spilling out, sprinting off in every direction.

"Dammit. Wait! Don't leave yet!" I shout.

"Forget it," Celia says. "They're not listening to you."

No kidding. I've totally lost control, if I ever had it in the first place. Jill and Celia are the only ones still with me, and we have no choice but to press on.

"I know the way out. Follow me." I toss the ring of keys on the ground and grip the blaster with both hands.

With all the noisy females flapping about, I expect to see guards looming down on us as soon as we step through the door. Somehow, miraculously, the coast is clear.

"This way." I wave at them, mentally reciting the directions that Griz made me memorize as we race down the hall. *Left, right, right, left, left, right, left, left.* I got this.

"Lass!"

No way! I scream to a halt and spin around. "Bruce!"

He barrels toward us, slowed only by a big-breasted crab on two legs, with wiggly hair that looks like matted seaweed and two huge eyeballs resting at the end of long antennae that sprout from her forehead. Despite her bright red color, he nearly mows her over at the intersection. Spinning around, she makes a high-pitched, mewling sound and clacks her pincers at him.

"Feck! Sorry . . . uh . . . lass. I didna' mean to hurt you," he says, his hands in the air as he takes a few steps back.

The crab girl twirls around and runs smack into a tall, thin purple girl with long, spindly arms and toothpick legs. They chatter what appears to be curses at one another, and then take off running again in opposite directions.

Bruce shakes his head and cautiously covers the rest of the distance between us. Flinging myself at him, I nearly knock him down. Screw it. I don't even care about the danger right now. Grabbing hold, I squeeze for all I'm worth, unable to stop the tears that come flooding.

"There, there, lass."

I close my eyes as my father holds me in his arms, arms that don't seem nearly as large as they used to after Griz. Still, they're full of love as he strokes my hair and offers soft words of comfort. Just as my tears begin to dry, he sets me on my feet and starts yelling at me.

"Now. What the blazes is going on here, Aine? You were supposed to wait for me back at the holding cells. And now, when I finally do catch up to you, they's crabbie lasses running this way and tattyboggles running that way. This was not the plan."

I wipe my nose on the back on my hand and grab his arm, pulling him back toward Jill and Celia who both appear to be in shock as they ogle Bruce.

"I know. I tried. They wouldn't listen to me. So, it's just me, Celia and Jill." I wave my hand toward them as an introduction. "Celia, Jill, this is my father, Bruce."

"That's your father?" Celia's jaw falls open, and I think I see a bit of drool dripping from her bottom lip.

To his credit, Bruce doesn't even flirt for once, seeming to understand that now is not the time. I'm glad because I'm not sure I can handle my father sidling up to a horny prostitute at this particular moment.

"Well, let's make for the exit and pray for the best." He tugs on my sleeve, dragging me forward a couple of steps. "Come on."

"Wait!" I stop short. "Where's Griz?"

I know something's wrong when Bruce sighs and gives me a serious look. He never looks at me seriously.

"That's why I'm late," he says. "He didn'a make it, lass. I'm sorry."

"What?"

Suddenly, it's like the madness around me falls away, and everything becomes a slow-motion film, a horror film. It's not the fact that we'd been abducted by aliens, or that we were being held on a spaceship by a giant lizard and his army. It's not even that I'm being auctioned as a sex slave or that we're on some bum-fuck Egypt of a planet in the asshole of the universe that I've never heard of that makes this whole thing so surreal. It's the thought of not having Griz here with me. He was the only thing that made this whole nightmare bearable. I need him.

"How?" Suddenly, nothing else matters except that. I have to know. Shaking Bruce, I scream at him. "Talk, Bruce! Tell me how he died!"

"Keep the heid, lass," he says as he reaches out and grips my shoulders. "He's not dead. That Beahl fella's got him locked up is all."

Oh, thank God. He's not dead. "Where? Where is he?"

Bruce squints at me, and for a moment, I'm afraid he's not going to tell me. Then, he must remember that I have the same stubborn Scottish blood as him, and that I'd stand here all day if I had to, because he finally relents. "He's back over yonder in the big baddie's quarters. At least, that's what Huberus told me."

I don't know who or what a Huberus is, but I need to get to Griz. Now.

"Tell me how to get there." I wrest my arm from his grasp and flip the safety switch on my blaster.

"Whoa, girlie. Yer aff yer heid if you think I'm letting you go after him."

"I'm not leaving without him, Pop. Tell me where he is. Or, I'll find him myself."

"And, what about them?" he says as he waves his hand toward Jill and Celia. "Who's going to get them out of here if you're off trying to rescue the alien?"

Suddenly, the lights in the hall flicker and flash blue. Another siren begins to wail overhead, making the situation seem even direr. Our time's up. Strangely, it's almost a relief, and I'm actually surprised it took them this long to figure out that we've all escaped our cells.

"Go!" Bruce growls and gives me a half-hearted shove toward the exit.

"No."

"Of all the . . . ." My father's whole body seems to deflate, and I almost feel sorry for him. "You're gonna be the death of me, lass."

"I can't leave him, Bruce. I can't." I shake my head, looking him in the eye and willing him to see the depth of my connection with Griz.

He nods, defeated, and waves an arm at the open hallway. "Just go, and take the lasses with you. I'll rescue the clawbaw, and we'll find you after we get out of here."

I debate for a moment, then realize my father is never going to back down on this one. All I can do is agree, and pray that I get them both back in one piece when this is over. Throwing my arms around his neck, I hug him as hard as I can.

"Thank you, Pop."

He pushes me away gently and plants a kiss on my forehead. "Scoot!"

# CHAPTER SEVENTEEN

Bruce

When I see Aine clear the end of the corridor, I stuff the blaster into the back of my pants and head off toward the big lizard's room, Beast or Bell or whatever his name is. Some kind of stupid alien name. If something's going to get screwed up, you can bet it's going to be one of those shite for brains aliens doing the screwing.

Suddenly, something with eight arms and four big, bouncy breasts attacks me, and I don't know whether to kiss it, slap it, or fondle it.

"Mmmeeee dwwweeeeeshabi chichicocko," it chants as I scrape it off me. Then, it tears off down the hall, a flurry of limbs flailing around its head.

I stare after it for a moment, scratching my head in wonder. "Of all the insane, boaby-headed . . . Oh! Haw."

As soon as I turn around, I smack into one of them mercs Griz was telling me about. The big, toad-faced twally-washer doesn't look too happy with me for running into him, and for a second, I don't ken if he's going to blast me or bonk me over the head with that club thing of his.

"Don't mind me. I'm just away for a dauner," I tell him, enjoying that blank look those aliens get when I start talking Scotty to them.

Unfortunately, I think I'll have to do better than that if I don't want to get clobbered by this knobdobber. "There's an orange-looking lass with eight arms and four giant tits that

129

just ran off down the hall that way," I tell him, pointing in the wrong direction.

I wasn't even sure the froggy fella could understand English, but that seemed to get his attention. I mean, he is a male, right? Anything with four giant tits will get our attention. His eyes are way too round to narrow at me, but I could tell they would be if he could have. He croaks what I take to be a warning, and I nod, skedaddling past him before he changes his mind.

I'm hauling ass down the corridor when I realize there aren't near as many guards roaming the hallways as I'd expected there to be. Least ways, not with all the flashing lights and these sirens wailing loud enough to wake the dead. I suppose it's a good thing because I can't seem to go five seconds without some half-naked female screaming past, flapping and squawking and making more noise than those blasted sirens.

Finally, I make it to the big baddie's room, only to find a dead lizard leaning up against the wall with a blood-drenched towel draped over his head. One of the four-armed, three-titted females stands over him, and she gives me a death glare as she brushes the back of her arm across her bloody lips. Like I'm going to feck with that?

"Quick! Get to the exit. I'll cover you," I shout, pointing down the hallway behind me. I nearly go boneless with relief when she actually heeds my advice.

Approaching cautiously, I take a closer look at the dead guard. He's half blocking the door, and he's got big chunks of flesh missing from his neck and arms. I don't know what this fella did to her, but she obviously didn't appreciate it. At least, she had the good grace to cover the poor bastard's face.

I stand there staring at the door for a minute, wondering for the first time how the hell I'm going to get my alien out of there. Well, not mine. Aine's alien, I guess. Looks like she wants him, after all. I suppose I could have done worse in the son-in-law department.

After see-sawing back and forth, I decide on the up-front, direct approach. Leaning over, I snatch the towel off the lizard's face and try not to gag. I place it over the blaster in my other hand and rap on the door.

All I can do is pray there's not an army inside there with him. Or, this is never going to work.

"What do you want?" a deep, croaky voice snarls through the door.

"Uh . . . I have a delivery," I tell him as I lift my toweled hand toward the peep hole. It sounds weak, even to me, but it's the best I could come up with spur of the moment. *Feck.* This is never going to work.

"What is it?"

Shite! I have no idea what to tell him, and the whole thing starts to piss me off. "How the feck should I know? That robot fella, Humorous, or whatever his name is, sent me."

Nothing happens for a minute, and I'm pretty sure he's about to blast me through the door. Just as I start to shuffle to the side, I hear locks clicking and clanking on the other side. I brace myself, adjusting my sweaty grip on the blaster as I pinch the towel between my fingers. I can't believe this actually worked.

As soon as the door swings open, I flip the towel in the air and pull the trigger. The big green bastard goes flying across the room, a hole the size of Montana right through his midsection. I leap inside, waving the gun from side-to-side looking for more baddies, the way they do on all those cop shows on the telly. I start to feel like a real tough son-of-a-bitch, and yeah, maybe I'm hamming it up just a wee bit.

I hear a bunch of muffled noises coming from the other room, so I elbow the door shut and make my way toward them. I move through the dark quarters, stealthy as a fecking ninja while I swivel my upper body left and right, pointing the blaster this way and that. Then, I see him. Our alien. Tied to a chair and gagged, bleeding all over the place.

"What the feck did they did to you, lad?" I keep the blaster ready in one hand as I untie his gag with my other.

"Hurry. They'll be right back," he says, as if that's going to make my hands stop shaking.

Refusing to set down my blaster, I finally manage to undo the bindings on his hands. He flings them aside and leans over to work on his feet. Once he's free, he pauses and looks down at me.

"Aine?"

"She's okay. Or, she was when I left her. Her and two other lasses were making their way to the exit."

"You shouldn't have left her," he growls as he takes off into the front room.

"Well, I sure as shite couldn't bring her with me, could I? And, the stubborn heifer wouldn't leave without you."

I watch as he flips over the guard with half his chest missing and relieves him of his blaster.

"You look like shite. Can you make it out of here?"

"Try and stop me," he growls.

Yeah, like I'm fecking crazy. The next thing I know, we're running down the corridors like our arses are on fire. At random intervals, the alien fires off a pulse or two, blasting guards out of our way like he's Rambo or something. Finally, I see light at the end of our tunnel, and it's at that very moment that all hell seems to break loose.

About a dozen laser pulses shoot past me, going off like fireworks all around us. My alien turns around and swings me in front of him. At first, I think the fecker is trying to use me as a shield, but then, I see the swarm of lizards behind us and realize the bastard just saved my life. I damn near feel guilty for being so mean to the fella.

We fly through the exit, my feet hitting solid ground for the first time in what seems like years, but I don't stop to kiss it. The sound of blaster fire cracks all around me, and bushes and trees disintegrate into smoking heaps of ash to my side.

"Split up!" he yells as he twists around and fires off a few pulses at the trailing army. "Go that way!"

I don't waste time arguing. I veer off, my feet leaving a smoldering trail behind me. I peer over my shoulder and catch one last glimpse of the alien. He's stopped running and stands there like a madman while white-hot pulses rain all around him. Then, he lets out some kind of ear-piercing war cry that has the hair on the back of my neck standing straight up. The last thing I see is him running straight for them, growling and firing off shots like crazy.

For a moment, I think about turning around to help him. But, if the guy wants to sacrifice his life to save me, who am I to ruin that for him? Anyway, I've always had a really strong sense of self-preservation. I put on more speed and haul arse out of there. I've done my part. He's alive and he's free. Now, it's up to him to stay that way.

# Chapter Eighteen

Aine

"Come with us!" I yell at the crazed girl with three breasts who's beating a path down the hall toward us and pinging back and forth off the walls like a pinball.

"It's no use," Jill says. "None of them understand a word we're saying."

She isn't the first girl we've tried to save. You'd think at least one of them would figure it out and fall in with us, but they just keep running around the ship in circles.

"Two more turns and there should be a door. Hurry." We take off in a sprint again, determined to get off this ship of horrors.

"There!" Celia points at the exit, and I put on a burst of speed.

The taste of freedom is sweet on my tongue as I hurl past the last noisy corridor. But then, the taste goes sour as a lizard in a blue waistcoat steps in front of the doorway and points a blaster at the three of us.

Fuck! I feel Jill and Celia slow behind me, and I know they're giving up, but I can't. I just can't do it. I know what awaits me if I fail.

Swinging the blaster in front of me, I scream like a mad banshee and half-ass aim as I squeeze the trigger. Blue Waistcoat Guy does a perfect swan dive to the left, somehow managing to evade my shots. Dodgy bastard. I fire off a few more pulses in his direction, and then a couple more at the door ahead of me that he tried to close.

"Don't stop," I scream behind me, praying the girls are keeping up. "Just keep going!"

I crash through the door like it's made of paper, just as two big guards rush at me from both sides.

Screw that! I don't stop. I feel their razor-tipped claws graze the back of my dress, and I kick up my speed another notch. Of course, they chase after me, and at least one of them is keeping up. The sound of his heavy footfalls is getting closer and closer until I can almost feel his breath on the back of my neck. Any second, he's going to knock me to the ground. He's got me.

Suddenly, a bright pulse of light zips right past my head. I screech, surprised by the near fatal shot, but don't stop. I pump my little legs as fast as I can, heading toward a grassy clearing ahead. Alarms blare in the distance, and I listen for the guard's weighty footsteps or the sound of his heavy breath behind me. I don't hear either one. Praying at least some of the other girls made it out, I glance over my shoulder, only to see a shower of pulses arcing toward me. Thank God, they all fall well short of their mark.

"Aine!"

My head snaps around, and I stumble, nearly crying at the sight. "Griz!"

I race toward him, my legs aching and nearly pushed to their limit. But that's nothing compared to the pain of my lungs, burning with every breath I take. Still, I don't stop until I crash into his arms.

"You made it," he proclaims, crushing me to him. "Thank the Goddess."

He kisses me about a thousand times as he raises his blaster and fires off a couple of pulses toward the ship. Then, he leans over and hefts me into his arms.

Taken off-guard by the surprise stoop and scoop, I let out a yelp and fling my arms around his neck. "What are you doing?"

"Rescuing you," he says, and then takes off running.

No, running is not a fair description. He shoots off like a bullet.

He moves so fast, I have to bury my face in the crook of his neck to keep the cold, biting wind from lashing at my eyeballs. It seems like we keep up this insane pace for hours until finally, he grinds to a stop, and I hear a door slam shut behind us. He's not even breathing heavy, but I'm panting like I just ran a five-mile marathon instead of being carried like a helpless princess. Suddenly, I realize I'm shivering so hard, my teeth are clacking together. I peek open my eyes, afraid the crazy Griz train is going to leave the station again any second.

"I think it's safe to rest here," he says, finally setting me on my feet. "Let me see if can get us some light."

I stand there quivering like jelly after a spanking—and, honestly, who hasn't spanked jelly before?—listening as he shuffles around in the dark. Suddenly, I hear the sound of a striking match, and bright light floods the room.

"Are you injured?" He looks at me closely now as he holds a weird-looking lantern in front of him.

Am I? I stand there like a twat while my brain tries to process the question, my chest heaving in and out, and my muscles locking up. Not waiting for me to reply, he starts running his hands all over me, lifting my arms and frisking me.

"Did they hurt you?"

I manage to shake my head.

"No. I'm okay," I finally say between chattering teeth, watching my breath come out in icy puffs. "But, oh my god. You're not."

Griz is covered in blood from head to toe, both his eyes swollen, cuts and gashes notched from his face and arms.

"What the hell did they do to you?" I reach out to touch him, but stop when I don't see a place on him that's not swollen or covered with blood.

"Nothing that won't heal, sweetling. Come here. You're freezing," he says, pulling me to him again and embracing me in his warmth.

I suspect he does it so I won't see his wounds and freak out, but I don't complain. His body gives off heat like a forest fire, and I'm all over him like Smokey the Bear.

"We need to stay here for a bit while they search for us," he tells me.

"Maybe they won't," I say, hope in my voice. "Maybe they've given up already."

Griz lets out a strained laugh. "Beahl will never let his prize female get away that easily. He'll use every resource he has."

Suddenly, I'm not feeling so safe anymore. I cling even harder to Griz for a few more minutes while I struggle to get my bearings. Once I can breathe somewhat easier, I push gently against his chest, rearing back to look up at him.

"Where's Bruce?"

"He got out," he says reassuringly. "But, we had to split up. I'm sure he's fine, though."

"What a relief." I sigh, feeling my shoulders sag. "What about the other girls? Jill and Celia. They should have been right behind me."

His eyes turn soft and sympathetic as he runs his hands up and down my bare arms. "I'm sorry, amavi. You were the only one I saw running toward the clearing."

"Dammit!"

For a moment, I see only red, unable to believe this turned into such a goat-fuck. Did any of them get out at all? How could I have failed so miserably? I nearly choke, flooded with guilt and shame. I got out. Bruce and Griz got out. And, we just left the rest of them behind. They were scared. They panicked. I should have helped them.

"There was nothing more you could have done," he says,

as if reading my thoughts. "You tried. You did your best."

Tears fill my eyes, and I stare at my feet, shaking my head. "Everything just got so fucked up. It was like chaos."

"Battles are always like that. You can't torture yourself with things you could have done or should have done. You just have to draw from your experience, learn what you can, and act on them next time. All warriors go through this."

"Born to lead revolutions, my ass," I scoff as I let my tears flow. I hear what he's saying, but I just don't care. My warrior days are done, and I don't plan on leading any more revolutions any time soon.

"Listen to me," he says, giving me a little shake and leaving me with no room for the pity party I'm trying to throw in my honor. "You are the granddaughter, nine times removed, of Robert the Bruce on your father's side. You're the niece, nine times removed, of Earth's legendary warrior, William Wallace, on your mother's side. If anyone was ever born to lead revolutions, it was you, amavi."

I raise my eyes to his, confused by his revelation. "How do you know that?"

"I looked it up," he says proudly.

"But, I failed," I whisper, not wanting to hear the words spoken aloud.

"No, you haven't. Not yet. We can still save them," he says as he whips a small knife from his pocket and flips it open.

"What are you going to do with that?" I watch as he pokes around, grazing his finger over the side of his already bleeding scalp.

"Let's pray Bruce is as good as he says he is," he tells me, his finger stilling over a spot behind his ear. "Go over there and hide behind those shelves. Don't come out until I tell you to."

"Why?" I don't like the sound of this.

"Because if this blows up, I want you clear of it," he says.

The fuck, you say? I figure I must look as horrified as I feel because his next words are much more measured.

"Don't worry. I don't think it will. If it was still active, I'm certain it would have already gone off. Beahl has surely triggered my device by now."

"Then, let me do it," I insist, because a few days of captivity have made me insane, apparently.

"Never," he growls, all scary-like, sapping the argument out of me. "Go."

He points to the shelves behind me, but my feet won't move. Instead, I lunge at him, wrapping my arms around his neck and kissing him anywhere my lips can reach while I sob like an ass.

"Amavi," he sighs, wrapping his arms around my waist. "It will be fine. I just don't want to take any chances. Not where you're concerned."

"But, you're already hurt," I whine, which has absolutely no bearing on the current topic, but upsets me, anyway.

"I will be healed by tomorrow, sweetling. I promise."

I nod, pressing my lips to his in a kiss that quickly becomes heated. Or, as heated as it can get with my nose leaking snot. His lips are pure fire, burning me from the inside out. I think he's scorched his initials into my very soul. I force myself to pull away finally, wiping my snot off his face and offering an apologetic smile.

"This will only take a minute," he tells me, his soft, warm eyes glistening with love and longing.

Slowly, I do as he says, tearing myself away and making my way behind two enormous shelves full of dusty clay jars and various odds and ends. I peek at him through a large crack in the wood, sweating in spite of the freezing cold. Once he's satisfied I'm out of harm's way, he begins.

I wince as he makes an incision behind his ear, pressing with his fingers and working something out from beneath the skin. When he holds a small cylindrical object on the tip of his finger, I breathe again.

"Can I come out?"

"Not yet," he says, opening the door and stepping outside. I wait impatiently for what seems like hours until he finally returns.

"Your turn," he says, and my stomach curls.

"That wasn't so bad now, was it?"

I'm tempted to punch him in the eye, but it's already nearly swollen shut from the beating Beahl's men gave him. I understood why he had to remove the chip from my head, but, dammit, it hurt.

He tucks his knife away, and for the first time since we got here, his sharp eyes take in the small structure where we've sought refuge.

"What is this place?" I ask tentatively.

I step out of his embrace and begin my own exploration. Floorboards creak and moan beneath my bare feet, and I've never longed for shoes so badly in my whole life. Weird-looking tools hang on walls carved from knotted, gnarly wood, and the sound of wind whistles in through a million tiny cracks. A window in the upper landing reveals the tops of enormous blue trees bending and swaying in the gale, and the sky outside begins to lighten with dawn, casting a pale green pall over the tops of several wooden stalls. Straw and hay lay strewn on both the upper and lower floors, and the scent of feces and animal sweat hangs thick in the air.

"Are we in a barn?"

As if on cue, a vibrating lowing sound comes from one of the stalls in the back.

"I'm not familiar with the term *barn*, but we are inside an animal dwelling," he tells me. "See?"

He points toward the back where a weird, hairy cow with

antlers stands staring at us as it chews on a mouthful of hay. Perched on its back is something that loosely resembles a chicken, but it's furry and has hooves, along with four eyes and fat, red lips. I'd bet a dollar it's a krustof.

Without provocation, the moose-cow lets out a menacing snort. I gasp and jump in front of Griz, raising my blaster, which until then, I hadn't realized I still held in my hand.

"No!" he shouts, and then chuckles as he reaches around me, pushing my arm back down. "It's only an old claffer. They are harmless." To prove it, he walks up to the beast and pats it on the neck. "Good femki," he coos.

Good femki, my ass. Not quite convinced, I keep a watchful eye on the creature, as well as the building's other unusual occupants as I dance from foot to foot on the cold floor. I'm afraid to stand still lest my feet freeze to it.

"So, what do we do now?"

Griz paces around the stalls, pulling what looks like a horse blanket out of one of them. He brings it to me, offering it with an apologetic smile.

"It may smell, but at least it's warm," he says.

Damn straight.

"I don't care if it smells like the ass end of a skunk right now," I proclaim as I take it from him and wrap it around me.

"Wait here a minute while I take a look around up there," he says, lifting his eyes to the loft.

I play stare-out with the hairy moose-cow while Griz pokes around upstairs, rustling around and dragging things across the floor.

"What are you doing?" I finally ask when my curiosity gets the best of me.

"Making a place for us to rest," he says. "It's ready. Can you climb up?"

I'm already at the top of the ladder before he finishes the question. Scooping me up, he lays me down on top of a straw bed that he's lined with some sort of large, smooth animal hide. I don't even want to think about the kind of beast it came from. But it's soft, and it's warm, and that's all I care about it right now.

The window is right overhead, and I watch as Griz skillfully maneuvers around it, peeking out occasionally.

"See anything?"

"No, and I hope it stays that way." He pulls off his thin, short-sleeved shirt and lies down next to me, rolling me to my side and spooning against me.

"Aren't you cold?" I ask, succumbing to a full-body shiver. Though, I suspect it's more from his bare skin pressed against my back than from the cold.

"It would take much more than this to make a Tarilean cold," he says proudly. "I'll keep you warm. We should try to get some rest while we can."

He spoons me tighter against him, and I'm firmly convinced I've somehow stumbled into Heaven.

On the other hand, there's not a chance in Hell I'm going to sleep. Not with him folded over me like a gum wrapper. My body is too aware of his, registering each and every infinitesimal move he makes, including the enormous, stiff body part that's currently pressing against my back.

Trying to ignore Griz's hard cock is like trying to ignore a full-scale Tarilean invasion on your front lawn. It's just not possible. The more I think about it, the more wicked my imagination gets, and soon, my entire body is on fire. I need him inside me. Then again, he feels awfully fucking big. I'm not totally sure it will even fit. I may be a virgin, but I've seen dicks before, and his seems to mock human biology. I wonder what he'd do if I touched it?

I will my hand to move, to reach behind me, and just grab it. But it refuses to do anything more than twitch. In the end, I chicken out, of course, opting instead to make him touch me.

# CHAPTER NINETEEN

Griz

I know if I let my hands caress her the way they want to, I won't be able to stop until I'm sheathed so far inside her, she will never again question who she belongs to. I've never fought a tougher battle, and if she wiggles that soft, sweet ass against my cock one more time, it's a battle I'm going to lose.

"Griz," she whimpers, and the sweet, husky sound of her voice sends a shiver up the entire length of my spine.

"Yes?" I nearly pant the word out.

"Touch me."

If my cock had seams, clearly, I would have burst through them now. I'm wound so tight, I don't even realize my arms are squeezing her until she squeaks. I force myself to calm, urging my instincts to back off so I can focus on my mate's needs.

"Like this?" I ask, gliding my hand over the soft curve of her hip and dipping it into the curly thatch of red hair between her thighs.

"Yes," she breathes, stretching her leg behind me and resting it on mine to give me better access.

I smooth my hand up her silky thigh and slide it beneath her gown. Slowly, my fingers skim the wet heat of her pussy, and I dip my fingers inside.

Shiest! I'll never make it through this alive.

Concentrating so I don't come in my pants again, I roll over and rest between her legs. She sighs as I work the thin gown over her head, pulling it past her outstretched arms. She looks up at me, her eyes heavy-lidded and full of desire, mewling as I flex my cock against her, rolling her nipple between my fingers.

"Claim me, Griz," she says so sweetly, I nearly lose my mind.

"Amavi," I groan. "I will pleasure you, but I don't want to claim you in an animal dwelling, lying atop a sheeta hide, with a blanket that smells like a claffer's ass."

Though, I'm not sure my cock agrees. My amavi deserves silk sheets, perfumed pillows and a plush warm bed. Not this.

"I don't care," she growls so fiercely, I cringe.

Before I know it, the little vixen has me tumbled on my back and we've swapped places. I stare in utter shock, held captive by her beautiful red locks that fall in wild waves across her shoulders and rest against her breasts. Plump, luscious breasts that heave in and out with every harried breath, their perky, pink tips just begging to be nipped and suckled. Then, she grinds her wet warmth against me, a wicked gleam in her eye.

"Amavi! Wait!"

"No! No more waiting," she says as her little fingers tug at the drawstring of my pants.

Suddenly, she's like a crazed butterbeast. For a click or two, I think maybe she's going to claim me! Before I can reason with her, before I can reason with myself, she has the hard length of my cock in her hot little hands, stroking it as she nestles in between my legs. My thoughts are so scattered, I fear I may never think straight again.

"Let's talk about this," I beg through gritted teeth, and then, my entire consciousness shatters, and I see stars dancing on the ceiling.

With no ceremonious petting or subtle clue of intent, my voracious mate devours me, sinking her wet, hot mouth over my cock and sucking so hard, my balls nearly cave in.

"Holy frizzuck!" I almost jump out of my skin.

Moaning, she bobs her head up and down, stroking me with both hands and cradling my shaft with her soft, wet tongue. I'm paralyzed. With a few strokes, my whole body tenses as it prepares for a fatal orgasm. And then, she stops. Pulling her mouth away with a loud pop, she sits up, licks her lips, and cups her beautiful breasts with both hands, squeezing her precious nipples and rolling them between her fingers.

"Claim me," she commands. "Now."

My mate is a demon, a wicked siren sent to punish me for every single misdeed and slight transgression I've ever committed or even thought about. My control vaporizes, dissipating in the air like a puff of smoke.

Growling, I grasp her hips and lift her to my face. She gasps, straddling me as I drag my tongue from her clit to her bottom hole and back again. I flick my tongue back and forth across her tiny bud as she whimpers and mewls, rocking frantically against my lips. I grip her hips tighter, holding her immobile as I ram my tongue into her slit.

She tastes like ValElysia, and I take my time drinking her. She bucks against my face and screams herself hoarse while I give her another long lick. Her body trembles, and I know she's close. Closing my lips around her little bud, I give it a nip, and then I suck. She comes screaming my name, her hips undulating, her hands clawing at my hair.

Tight in the grip of the mating frenzy, I flip her over, tucking her beneath me even as she's still pulsing from her climax. Her glazed eyes center on me as I scoop my arms beneath her knees and lift her hips, pressing my cock to her entrance. Then, I look into her warm, half-lidded eyes and give her my solemn vow.

"I've waited my whole life for you, my beautiful, warrior

145

princess. You are my fated mate, my amavi compar. My hearts are yours and yours alone. I belong only to you and you to me. Forever."

She gasps as I nudge the head of my cock inside her, gently pressing forward until I meet the resistance of her maidenhood.

"Don't stop," she pleads. "Please, don't stop."

I have no intention of stopping. The roof could come down around us, and I wouldn't stop. I reach around, flicking and pinching her nipples as I rock my hips against her. Then, I squeeze them. Hard.

She screams, and I pound my cock inside her, taking her virginity and her innocence, and sheathing myself to the hilt in her hot, tight channel until I'm sure I'll die from the bliss. Suddenly, I feel my wounds begin to heal—the swelling around my eyes recedes, bones knit back together, and strength returns to my muscles. But the restorative powers of an amavi compar are no more than a fleeting thought right now.

Though it strains every nerve in my body, I force myself to stay still while she gasps and huffs, trying to breathe through the pain of her lost maidenhood. I stroke her hair and plant soft, encouraging kisses on her cheeks until I feel her hips begin to move against me.

"Are you all right, my love?"

"Yes," she says breathlessly. "Please. Don't stop."

I don't intend to. I pull almost all the way out and gently slide back in, watching to make sure I'm not hurting her. But the look on her face is pure, undiluted bliss, so I do it again, harder this time, driving a soft moan from her lips, and fueling my fervor as ecstasy spirals through me.

All the while, I can feel myself healing, drawing strength with every thrust of my hips and stroke of my cock. My orgasm perches nearby, ready to reach out and take me at any second. My balls tighten almost painfully, and I can feel my cock begin to swell as I rocket my hips against her. I can't hold back anymore.

"Aine," I groan.

"Griz!" she answers with a scream, and her inner muscles begin to clench, spasming around me so tightly, I nearly go blind.

My hips stutter, and I shout out my orgasm to the world as my seed jets and pumps inside her. My toes curl, my teeth grit, and my eyeballs roll back in my head. Her pussy squeezes all around me, pulling me in even deeper, and I'm afraid I might actually pass out. But, right now, there is nothing else in the world, nothing but me and my mate, and this indescribable rapture.

My cock swells at a staggering rate until suddenly, I feel the mating lock snap into place, setting off another violent torrent of orgasms. My fangs lengthen and ache, my body driven only by instinct as I drive them into the tender skin of my mate's neck.

Aine screams, her head thrown back in wild abandon as her pussy begins to clench and squeeze all over again, milking the very soul from my body.

Her blood is like the sweetest nectar, feeding my frenzy and fueling my bliss. Finally, I force myself to stop, detracting my fangs and licking the little beads of blood that pool around my mark, the evidence of my claiming.

"Mine!" The word rips out of my throat as another wave of pleasure rolls through me. My hips jerk and bump against the cradle of her thighs as I hold her protectively beneath me.

Finally, I bury my face in Aine's neck, surrounded by her scent, made even sweeter by a light sheen of sweat between us. I shower her with gentle kisses up and down her jaw as I stroke her all over. My hips jerk involuntarily every few clicks as my cock jettisons more seed into her, shooting white hot sparks of pleasure through my whole body every time.

"Griz?"

"Yes, my love," I whisper between kisses.

"How can you still be . . . you know . . . doing that?"

"Doing what?"

She sighs as a blush steals up her neck and lands squarely on her cheeks.

"You know. Coming in me," she finally whispers.

My sweet, innocent little mate. She knows nothing of mating, not even this. Then again, she's had no mother to prepare her, and the thought makes my protective instincts flare.

"It's the mating lock, sweetling."

"What's a mating lock?"

I try to hide my smile. Though, in all honesty, her lack of mating knowledge almost borders on neglect. To not know a mating lock at her age? Unheard of.

"My body recognizes its true mate," I explain. "So, when we joined, it triggered the mating muscles around the base of my cock, locking us together, and spawning multiple climaxes."

I pause, shuddering and flexing my hips as another wave of pure pleasure barrels through me.

"Will it do this every time we . . . you know?" she asks, her eyes round with trepidation.

I chuckle. "Mate? No, sweetling. Only the first time we join. It's my body's way of ensuring that it's seeding you properly."

Dropping my face to her breast, I draw her nipple into my mouth, sucking and nipping as the next climax ebbs through me. She gasps, clenching around me and drawing out my pleasure until I'm panting and sweating once again. At this rate, we may not leave here for days.

"What do you mean, 'seeding me properly?'"

I shake my head in disbelief. Oh, my sweet, innocent

princess. "When I release my seed inside you, amavi, it ferti-
lizes your eggs. This is how we will make younglings, and
you—"

"What?"

She nearly tosses me off her trying to get up, and would
have succeeded were we not literally stuck together by the
mating lock. As it is, the only thing she succeeds in doing is
nearly ripping off my cock.

"Ow! Ow! Stop that!" I push her back down, holding her
in place with my hips. "What are you doing? What's wrong
with you?"

# CHAPTER TWENTY

Aine

Deep breaths. Deep, calming breaths.

"Griz, are you saying that you can get me pregnant?"

He looks at me strangely for a moment. "Aine, I understand why Bruce would not feel comfortable speaking to you about mating, and maybe not even details about the mating lock. But, how could you not know where younglings come from? They aren't really left on doorsteps by korstlas, sweetling."

So, first of all, I have no idea what a korstla is. Secondly, he's not even human. I mean, a fish and a bird can love each other, but where will they live kind of thing . . . . Right? Surely, we aren't compatible . . . in that way. Then, again, with the amount of sperm he's pumping into me, he could probably impregnate a herd of human females.

With that thought, he starts coming again. His cocks swells and jerks inside me, and I can feel his hot sperm surging into me. I moan and grind against him like a two dollar hooker. I simply have no shame.

On second thought, would it really be so bad to be pregnant with Griz's baby? *Right now, yes!* I have another quick flash of panic, my thoughts coming to me in little staccato images. *Pregnant. Baby. Pirates. Spaceship. Hairy Cows.* This is no time to think about starting a family.

"Griz, I can't get pregnant right now. You have to stop. Pull it out."

He starts laughing. Laughing!

"Sweetling," he finally says, stroking my burning cheeks. "There's no way to stop a mating lock. It only happens once in a male's lifetime, and there's nothing we can do except ride it out. Until my body deems that you're properly seeded, it will not cease."

There's a lot about that statement that freaks me out. I try to focus on one piece at a time, though. "It only happens once in a whole lifetime?"

"Yes. One amavi, one mating lock."

Then, it hits me over the head like a ball peen hammer.

"Amavi. You call me that all the time. What does it mean?"

His eyes sparkle, and his luscious lips curl into a beautiful smile. "You are my amavi compar, my fated mate."

Slowly, it sinks in. I'm his only one. He's my only one. My heart melts as another spasm hits my pussy, setting off delicious little tingles and liquefying my brain. I close my eyes and shiver. I can't do anything about it, so I might as well lie back and enjoy.

"I'm guessing a cigarette and a hot shower are out of the question. So, what now?"

I watch as Griz does his best to wipe away the gallon of "seed" that's stuck to half his body before pulling on his pants. The good news, though, is that he's one-hundred percent healed now. All those nasty cuts and bruises? That swelling around his eyes? Gone. Poof. Apparently, my pussy has some kind of magical healing power. Who would have ever thought? Fortunately, it only works on him.

"The first thing we have to do is find you some warmer clothes and some foot coverings," he says, nodding at my bare feet.

"How are we going to do that?"

"There should be a small town not far to the west of here,"

he says, tugging his shirt over his head. "I have enough credits on me to get us some food and warm clothing."

"Thank goodness." I'm more relieved than I thought I'd be to hear that we're not flat broke. Plus, a hot meal and some warm, dry clothes sound like pretty darn good right now. Well, as long as I can shower first. Griz isn't the only one covered in alien jizz.

"Then what?" I probe.

"There should be a coms station in town. I need to contact my people. I can have them meet the ship at Janyx, and, hopefully, find my dam."

"Do you think they can?"

"What? Find my dam?" His mouth smooths into a flat line. "I don't know, but I know without a doubt that my cousin will try. He will send warriors."

"How long before Beahl's ship gets to Janyx?"

"About two cycles," he says.

I let my face go blank. "What is a cycle? A day? A month?"

"About one Earth month."

"So the girls have to stay with those . . . those monsters for two more months?"

He sighs, and I can tell he's as frustrated as I am. Then, I feel guilty for nagging him. I mean, we've only been mated for a few hours, and already I've turned into a yapping shrew.

"I'm sorry. I know you're trying," I say, feeling ashamed when I think of how badly he was hurt just a few hours ago trying to help us escape. I fold my arms around him, nearly purring as he strokes my hair.

"I will certainly do everything I can to retrieve them sooner, amavi. Without a ship, there's just not a lot more I can do. If I know Horok, though, he'll contract peacekeepers to try and intercept them while he goes after my dam. Still, it's unlikely they'd be able to locate them before they reach Janyx. Even if they did, with all the corruption and bribery that goes on around the slave trade there, it's hard to say whether peacekeepers would even be effective."

Dirty peacekeepers?

"Also, Beahl's no fool. He'll change up his route now, and with the ship's cloaking capabilities, it'll be like finding a nistle in a huif stack. Right now, let's just focus on the situation with your sire," he says as he makes his way over to the loft ladder.

What situation with my sire?

"What? Why? Is he in danger?"

Shit! There's probably big, hairy, meat-eating yaks running around out there with hoofed chickens on their backs, trying to eat my pop at this very moment. And here I've been matelocked with an alien for the past three hours. I leap for my blaster and nearly scrabble over the top of him trying to get down the ladder.

"What? No!" He laughs. "This is probably the safest planet in the galaxy."

My pulse ratchets down a notch or two. "Thank goodness. But then, why are we worried about Bruce?"

"Because it's also one of the largest planets in the galaxy, more than half of it dense, undeveloped woodlands. He could be anywhere. If we don't find him before night fall—"

"There's a town, you say?"

"Yes. Probably just a few clicks to the west, but Bruce was heading north the last time I saw him."

Well, fuck. As cold as it is here in the daytime, I can only imagine the temperatures at night. He was in short-sleeves, too, and if he doesn't find a place to hide in like we did, he could freeze.

"Should we head north, then?" I don't know what the hell to do now.

"We have to get you some food and warm clothing first. You can't search for him with bare feet."

He's right. Dammit.

"Here." He clenches the smelly blanket tight around me, and as offensive as it is, I'm still thankful to have it. I just hope Bruce has one, too. I snuggle into it as we head off toward the town.

It's amazing how slowly thirty minutes crawl by when your toes are frozen and you think you may have chipped a few teeth from all the chattering they've done. I wait quietly in the corner for Griz, alone with my smelly blanket, trying to avoid people in the little coms station. It's not difficult to do. I stink so bad, anyone who comes near scrunches their nose and takes off in the other direction. I'm starting to get a complex.

"There. That's done," Griz says, wrapping his arm around me and leading me outside.

"You reached them?"

"Yes. My cousin is putting together a team of our best warriors even as we speak," he says, but his voice lacks any real conviction.

"I'm sure they'll find your mum," I tell him, trying to project as much optimism as I can.

He takes my hand in his, squeezing it, and leads me down a rocky pathway in front of the coms station.

"According to the clerk, there's a hotel two buildings down on the left. You can take a bath while I go out and find you some clothing. After that, we'll head out and look for Bruce."

"I could really use a bath and some warm clothes," I tell him, nearly weeping at the thought.

But then, the sound of laughter grabs my notice, and a familiar sight catches my eye. It's a freaking pub, and I'd recognize that boisterous laugh anywhere. I grind to a halt, nearly giving Griz whiplash.

"What? What is it?" he asks, his head swiveling this way

and that as he grasps the blaster tucked neatly into his waist-band.

"First, we go there." I point to a building across the bright, lemon-colored street.

The building itself looks like an old West saloon, right down to the swinging-hinged doors in front and the large wooden wrap-around porch. There's even a rocking chair sitting by itself, rocking back and forth in the wind as if trying to tempt an occupant.

I don't hang around for Griz's response. I'm tired. I'm cold, and I'm hungry. And now, I'm pissed. Not to mention, I'm running around town in what is basically a thin, flimsy nightie in the midst of what appears to be winter with bare feet and no underwear and wrapped in what looks and smells like a dirty horse blanket. All the while worried sick about my father, imagining him curled up under a shrub in the woods freezing to death. I'm in no mood now to have to pull him out of yet another drinking establishment on yet another planet.

I march my bare feet and naked, freezing ass across the smooth lemony surface of the weird-looking street, across the big, wooden porch, and fling the swinging doors aside like I'm Wyatt Earp at the O.K. corral. All conversation inside ceases immediately, and every head in the joint turns to look at me. Except one.

Snarling like a rabid animal, I trudge toward the only dark haired, middle-aged, half-soused human male sitting at the bar. He holds onto a glass of something that looks like carrot juice, but I know it's not while he talks to a short, squatty blob of purple fuzz with black lips and red eyeballs.

"I'm telling you," he goes on. "They wuz flat tearin' the tartan and not paying a bit of mind to any goings on around them. I got the drop on all three afore they even ken what was happening." He laughs and claps his hand against his knee. "You should have seen them peely-wally aliens when I—"

I reach out and grab Bruce by the ear. The fuzzy little purple guy lets out a loud squeak, along with a nasty, foul odor, as I drag Bruce off the barstool.

"Oy!" he shouts, twisting out of my grip and turning to face off with his latest abuser. "Aine!"

The look on his face is almost comical. I prop my fists on my hips and tap my foot against the wooden floorboards, looking like the stereotypical Earth female come to drag her inebriated father out of a bar for the tenth time this month.

"I can explain, lass," he says, and then, stops suddenly, raising his face and sniffing at the air until his nose comes to rest right in front of my chin. He stiffens and pinches his nostrils together. "Holy mother of . . . Aine, you smell like a stopped-up bucket in July."

Angry as I am, it still makes me wince. What girl wants to be told she smells like a dirty outhouse? Especially in front of her new mate and a room full of witnesses.

"Well, maybe some of us have been forced to hide up the ass-end of a hairy yak while you've been in here all warm and toasty, drinking and recounting tales of all your heroic deeds!"

Despite my anger, I can feel more tears threatening to spill down my cheeks. I've never cried so much in my life.

"I didn'a mean to hurt your feelings. Come here, lass," he says, looking penitent as he spreads his arms wide.

I teeter on the edge of hugging him and punching him in the nose. I tip over on the side of hugging him. Just barely. It's only then that I notice the noise in the bar pick back up again.

Finally, I wipe the stray tears from my face and give him a hairy eyeball.

"I'm at the end of my rope," I tell him. "I honestly can't take anything else, Bruce. I need to lie down somewhere and just close my eyes for a few minutes so I can pull myself together."

"Come on. We're getting a room across the street," Griz tells him as he steps behind me. His strong, warm hands on my shoulders instantly make me feel better.

We turn to head for the exit when a big, brutish fellow, who looks kind of like a Black Angus bull standing on two legs, yells at us from behind the bar.

"Hey! Who's paying his tab?"

I narrow my twitching eyes at Bruce, and he turns away so fast, I feel the breeze against my cheek.

"I've got this," Griz says and steps back to the bar to pay the check.

"I can't believe you did that," I snap at Bruce. "What if we hadn't come along? What would you have done then?"

It's about this time that things start getting loud over my left shoulder.

# CHAPTER TWENTY-ONE

Griz

"What do you mean, you don't accept Tarilean mekkas? Who doesn't accept Tarilean mekkas?" I glare at the Brahmanian bartender.

"We don't," he says, pointing to a sloppy, handwritten sign hanging above the bar.

"Fine. Here." I dig my credit chip out of my pocket and slap it on the counter.

The cagey beast stares at it for a click and then points above the bar again. "Read the sign."

Sure enough, right under "We do not accept Tarilean mekkas" is another sentence scrawled in big, red letters that says "We do not accept credit chips." I heave an aggravated sigh. Maybe I can reason with this claffer-headed ass.

"Look, we've barely managed to fight our way out of a really bad situation and come away with our lives. We just want to get back home. Can't you cut us a break and make an exception this one time?"

He snarls and points to the sign again, and I have to squint, straining my eyes just to make out the tiny letters at the bottom—*No exceptions*.

I wish I had my sword. Or my staff. Either would do right now as I glare at the obstinate tapster. I slap my hand over the credit chip lying on the bar and push it toward him.

"Take it or leave it," I shout.

The angry bartender leaps across the bar and grabs me by my shirt collar. Somehow, it's gotten past my attention that he's at least a good foot taller than me and twice as broad. Well, okay, then.

No matter. I'm about to kick his ass when suddenly, there's a loud crash, followed by a shower of tinkling glass. I stare at him, stunned, as his eyeballs roll up in his head and he slumps to the floor in a heap of limp fur. It's only then that I spy my tiny mate, standing on the bar behind him, with the remains of a kocho bottle in her hand.

"Nobody touches my mate!" she informs the rest of the bar's frozen patrons. Only after meeting each of their eyes does she drop the remnants of the bottle, hop down off the bar, and pick up her filthy blanket.

"Let's go," she says to me firmly.

Who the Haelic is this female? I see Bruce standing next to a table of Wharfles, his shoulders slumped, and his eyes riveted to the floor in a submissive pose. Taking his lead, I don't argue. I snatch my credit chip off the bar and toss a handful of mekkas in its place.

Quickly, we make our way toward the exit, and we're almost there when a huge, blue male from Aurelia IV steps into the aisle and blocks our way. *Frizzuck!* Aurelia IV is known throughout the galaxy as the home world of the most feared and ruthless mercenaries in the universe.

My fingers crawl toward the blaster beneath my shirt, and I'm working out my plan to take the male down when I hear a low, reverberating growl coming from the direction of my mate. The hairs on my arms stand straight up, and I see Bruce cringe, all the color bleeding from his face.

"Look, fella. You doona ken what you're messing with here," he whispers, nervously cutting his eyes at Aine. "She gets crazy when she's like this."

"I'll help you," the merc rumbles, and we all stare at him expectantly. He doesn't say another word. Nothing else. Just that.

My mate steps forward, her little fists resting on her curvy hips as she cranes her neck back and looks the nasty killer in the eye. "How?"

"Not here," he rasps. "Some place where there aren't so many ears."

I watch as my mate eyes him coolly. Then, she nods. "Okay. Come with us."

Wordlessly, we all follow Aine across the street to the hotel. I trot, trying to catch up with her as she enters the front lobby and sweeps to the front desk.

"Do you take mekkas or credit chips?" she asks.

A small female from the O'oora system smiles with one set of her lips and purses the other ones. "Of course."

"Good," my mate says with a nod. "We need a room, then. With a hot shower," she adds.

She finally looks at me, her eyes softening just a smidge.

"You take care of this, and I'll take care of them," she says, jerking her chin toward Bruce and the merc.

I nod enthusiastically, still too afraid to speak. I could say the wrong thing and set off an intergalactic incident. She lifts to her tiptoes and gives me a peck on the cheek, and I catch a glimmer of my real mate, the sane, not so scary one, before she turns and heads toward the two hulking males staring at each other across the room.

I slide my credit chip to the O'oora female and instruct her to send up some food for the three of us. The Aurelian can fend for himself. After taking care of the bill, I wave at Aine to follow me, and we all head up the stairs to room two-seventeen.

"All right, then. Tell us how you can help," I say to the Aurelian merc as we all file into the small sitting area.

"I heard you escaped from the Lizentines," he says matter-of-factly, ignoring my demand as he plops down onto one of the worn armchairs.

My blood goes cold, sure that we've been led into a trap. Pushing my mate behind me, I know it's too late to do anything about it now. If the merc decides to take us back for a reward, there's nothing we'll be able to do to stop him.

"So?"

"Well, you two are said to be dead or gravely injured," he says, cutting his eyes between me and Bruce. "But, there's already a contract with the bounty hunters for your return. A nice fat reward, too."

His laser gaze locks onto my mate, and my hand grips tightly around my blaster. Frizzuck. I knew it.

"And, your intentions?" Bruce speaks up, glaring at the oversized assassin, though the merc is twice as big as him, even sitting down and slumping in the chair.

Not for the first time, I'm impressed with the courage these humans possess. I can't believe my incredible fortune to have one as my mate, and I'll die before I let any harm come to her.

The merc sneers and lights up a maristachi cigarette. The purple smoke curls around him lazily and then wafts through the room like a toxic finger. I cough and wave my hand back and forth in front of my face. A person can get high off those fumes alone.

"Relax. I hate Lizentines. I have no intention of helping those cowardly parasites," he declares, and then takes a long draw of the potent weed. "I just want the bastard that took my little sister."

Aine gasps and claps her hand over her mouth. "Oh my god. I'm so sorry. We tried to free everyone."

"Yeah I heard," he says, narrowing his eyes first at me, then at Bruce as if to imply that we're incompetent. Unbidden, a growl sneaks past my lips.

"Wait a minute. Why are they supposed to be dead?" My mate glances nervously between me and her sire.

"He must have set off our devices. For all he knows, we're

both lying dead on a sidewalk somewhere, five stones lighter without our heads. Ten stones, in his case." I look at Bruce. "Which reminds me, I need to remove your implant."

Bruce grimaces, but doesn't argue. Instead, he nods in agreement, and I turn my attention back to the merc.

"Anyway, I still don't understand how you think you can help us."

"I have an offer for you." His lips curl into a half-smile, and he shifts his eyes back to my mate. "I'll help you with your little contract problem, and you help me get my sister back."

I don't like the way he looks at Aine. Still, we're in a bad spot here, and I'd love to get my hands on Beahl. I scratch my cheek as I consider his proposal. Offers from Aurelians can be tricky things. You can never be sure if you'll end up ahead of the game or indebted to a ruthless mercenary for the rest of your life. I open my mouth to question him further, but I'm interrupted before I can get a word out.

"Deal!" Aine blurts.

My head snaps around so fast, I get dizzy. *It's probably from the maristachi.* I gawk at my over-zealous mate as she shoves her hand in the air toward the stranger. I remember Bruce doing the same thing to Huberus. The merc stares at it with a cool curiosity, and then looks at her, his eyes questioning.

"Where I come from, people shake hands when they make a deal," she explains.

He grunts. "Where I come from, people kill people who don't honor them."

My mate frowns at him, and I quickly intervene, slipping my arm around her shoulders and guiding her toward the small refresher in the back.

"Sweetling." I speak softly to her so the others can't hear. "Why don't you take a nice, long soak in the tub? I'll run over and pick up some clean garments for you while you bathe, and when I get back, our food should be here."

Thankfully, she agrees, the lure of a bath too much for her to resist, and I return to the living room as soon as I hear the door lock and the water running. To my horror, Bruce and the merc are already plotting by the time I return, Bruce sprawled casually on the couch, and the merc splayed out with one leg draped over the chair arm.

"I didn't catch your name," I rudely interrupt.

"I didn't give it to you," the merc replies offhandedly. "But I'm Epherus Zinto. My friends call me Eff, but you can call me Epherus."

"Well . . . *Epherus*. I thank you for your kind offer, but I'm afraid we're going to have to decline," I tell him politely.

It's just not worth the risk to my mate to fall in league with an Aurelian assassin. They simply can't be trusted.

He drags his leg off the arm of the chair and sits up straight, bringing his eyes nearly level with mine. My body goes rigid as I watch the two deadly horns on top of his head rotate slowly toward me. Sharp, poisonous barbs normally hidden beneath the tough, blue leathery skin of his forearms begin to extend and lengthen as he brushes back his vest to reveal a pair of handheld molecular disbanders.

Well, shiest. He scowls at me for a moment, and I feel my fingers twitching toward my blaster. Then, the blue bastard smiles, though it's anything but friendly, and grants us an intimidating display of long, pointy teeth and needle-sharp fangs.

"Fortunately for you," he says as he stubs out what's left of his cigarette on his boot heel and pops the rest of it in his mouth. "My deal is with the female."

"That female is my mate," I growl.

"That female is my daughter," Bruce snarls, probably more at me than the assassin.

Epherus takes in the situation between me and Bruce and chuckles. "And, I've got no problem with her. So long as she stands by the deal we made."

I slide my gaze to Bruce who's now perched on the edge of his seat, coiled and ready to strike at a moment's notice.

"Fine." I sigh in defeat, not wanting to chance any harm coming to him or my mate. Or, to me, either, for that matter. As much as my ego hurts by the admission, I'm not sure I could take him. "How do you propose we proceed?"

"I have a ship. She's fast. If you know where they're headed, we can cut them off."

"He'll be heavily cloaked," I tell him.

The merc shrugs, smirking. "Just get me in the general vicinity. I can use my ship's photon fields to track the plasma exhaust from his ship. Or, if his ship is big enough, and I think it is, my tachion detection grid will pick him up."

Holy claffer. I've never heard of a civilian vessel with that kind of advanced weaponry and technology. Last I heard, it was only available to select intergalactic military warships.

"And, what will we do then? Once we cut them off?" Bruce asks.

"I'm going to board them," the merc states rather flippantly, confirming my suspicion that he's a raving lunatic.

"You're what?" Bruce stands and shakes his head at Epherus. "What kind of huddy havers are you spouting?"

"There's more than seventy-five crew members, Ranan mercs and soldiers for hire on board that craft," I clarify.

Epherus pulls out another cigarette and taps it thoughtfully against his boot heel. "Roughly what I estimated. Won't be a problem."

I'm tempted to call "claffer shiest," but then again, Aurelians aren't referred to as perfect mass murderers for nothing.

"I know where they're going," I tell him. "But I'm boarding the ship with you."

"Whatever." He shrugs and lights another cigarette. "Your funeral."

# Chapter Twenty-two

Aine

"Damn. When Epherus says he has a ship, he's not just whistling Dixie," I tell Griz as Epherus' craft comes into view.

We walk hand in hand toward the sleek, shiny ship with Epherus leading the way and Bruce trailing closely behind, gawking at all the strange-looking aliens arriving and departing from the station. I'm practically strutting, my brand-new boots shining beneath the bright florescent lights, and the rest of me nice and toasty in my brand-new duds.

The sleek black pants I'm wearing have the airy feel of cotton, but the look of leather. Almost pleather, but softer. My pale grey top is made from a fine, sturdy fabric and appears to be some kind of enhanced thermal. It's virtually molded itself around me, squeezing in and plumping up all the right places. What's more, it's so warm, I don't even need a coat. Griz thought of everything, even picking me up a holster for my blaster, which is now strapped to my thigh. I feel like a right badass.

"I'm not familiar with this Dixie, but Aurelia IV is known for producing the best quality spacecraft," he says, a thoughtful look on his handsome face. "Probably because they also produce the best quality assassins who often need to get the Haelic out of town fast after a mission."

Epherus might not be the most savory character, but I'll take my chances. He's big and scary with expensive toys and deadly skills from what I can see. Exactly what I want when I'm going lizard hunting.

Craning my neck, I look over the sleek, sharp edges of the impressive ship in front of us. I don't know much about space travel, but if we were riding in a Buick before, we've definitely upgraded to a Cadillac now.

"Well, let's hope it's as fast as it looks," I remark.

"Beahl's ship is big and bulky, built for hauling cargo, not outrunning pirate ships. We'll catch up quickly," Griz promises me for about the tenth time since I woke and learned that Epherus had a ship.

Needless to say, I wasn't happy. The bath and the food were terrific, the new clothes a dream. And, make no mistake, the nap left me totally rejuvenated. But now, we're almost a day behind Beahl. I can't imagine catching up to them now, regardless of Griz's reassurance.

When I got out of the shower at the hotel, everyone was gone, but there was a hot meal on a covered dish waiting for me, and I was starving. After devouring my plate of . . . whatever it was, I wasn't sure without ES Four Three Nine there to tell me, I stretched out on the bed and fell fast asleep. I appreciate Griz letting me rest, but I'd much rather have been in the air, going after Jill, Celia and the others.

"This way."

Epherus' deep, gravelly voice rolls over my skin and makes me shiver, not in a good way.

Everything about Epherus screams "dangerous killer." Even his biology and physique, wide as a damn bulldozer with his fangs and pointy teeth, and those long quill things on his arms. I stick close to Griz and keep a sharp eye on Bruce, who has a way of making even virtuous people want to kill him. No telling how long before he pushes an assassin with no moral compass to the edge. I'm surprised he's made it this long.

Epherus comes to a full stop in front of the gleaming hull of the ship, staring straight ahead.

"Captain requests access," he says, and a red beam of light promptly crawls across his face.

A seamless opening appears on the exterior surface of the craft, and he breezes through it.

"Come," he growls over his shoulder, and I'm tempted to bark like a dog.

Nevertheless, we follow, Bruce and me gawping as we make our way down the narrow passages. All around me, smooth, shiny metal makes up the surface of the interior. Mostly cold, grey and clinical, I get excited when I see a splash of warm hues adorning the walls of the bridge just ahead of us.

Walking onto the bridge feels more like stepping inside a university planetarium. A lone chair sits in the middle of a raised platform in the center of the cavernous area. One long window wraps around the entire expanse of the room, making it seem even larger and giving it a three-dimensional effect. I fight back a childish urge to yodel to see if it echoes.

Beneath the window in the front is a long row of consoles and control panels, a few chairs scattered up and down the length.

Epherus wastes no time, striding to one of the consoles where he flips an array of switches, turning knobs and jabbing buttons. The ship powers up, and I feel only a slight vibration beneath my feet.

"You two," he says, pointing at me and Bruce. "Sit over there, and strap in."

I glance at Bruce, who appears to be just as spaced out as I am. Quickly, I glean that he's not going to provide a lot of support here, so I make my own way toward the long line of folding chairs against the wall beside the dais. Thankfully, Griz takes my arm and guides me to a spot where I have a good view of the central operations area.

"Sit here, sweetling, and I'll buckle you in," he says, kissing me lightly atop my head.

I do as he says, getting a little excited as he fumbles with the buckle between my legs. His warm hands so near my greedy core, coupled with the memory of this morning, causes me to gush like a horny teenager. He pauses, sparing me a heated look as I give him my best come hither eyes nearly forgetting that we're not alone.

"Ahem." Bruce clears his throat and scowls at Griz while I blush furiously.

Griz scowls back at him as he snaps my final buckle into place.

"She's my fully-bonded mate," he snaps childishly at Bruce.

I give my head a little shake at Griz, praying that Bruce doesn't know what a fully-bonded mate is. My eyes plead with him silently, as I really don't want to hash out the details of our relationship right now in front of my cock-blocking father and the psychotic killer who's now turned around in his chair and giving us his undivided attention.

"I ain't seen no preacher or attended no ceremony," Bruce snips back, narrowing his eyes at Griz threateningly.

*Oh, shit.*

"I have said my vows before Aine and the Goddess, and we have—"

"Got to go now!" I blurt before he can finish that last sentence. "Get us out of here," I shout at Epherus, who's laughing so hard, he has tears in his eyes.

He spins around in his chair and mumbles, "Humans."

Griz gives my harness one last tug, and seemingly satisfied that I won't fly out of my seat, strolls toward the chair closest to Epherus and sits down.

"Ever driven a Mercurus Four-Thousand?" Epherus asks Griz.

Griz gives the console a good once-over while he straps himself in.

"No, but it doesn't look too difficult," he replies, flipping a couple of the switches and reaching over his head to depress a serious-looking red button with weird squiggly lines on it.

I swell with pride, and no small measure of lust, as I watch my impressive mate. Then, I notice Bruce glaring at me from the corner of my eye. I cough and clear my throat, diverting my eyes to the front window.

Almost fluidly, the ship begins to rise up off the platform and drift forward, slowly gaining height as we go. Within seconds, we're already in the clouds.

"Hang on," Griz says. "He's about to engage the hyperdrive."

He doesn't have to tell me twice. I grip the chair arms so hard, my knuckles turn white. Then, I say farewell to my stomach as we launch into a death hurtle straight into outer space. Finally, once my liver has crawled half-way up my throat and my puckered butthole has ripped an impressive hole in the chair cushion beneath me, we begin to slow, and the ship seems to level out. Admittedly, the whole thing wouldn't have been nearly as bad were it not for the loud screaming in my ears the entire time. Once I realized it was me and stopped, it was a lot better.

"Coordinates?" Epherus asks, and Griz rattles off a series of digits longer than my birth date and social security number combined.

After a few more tense and harried minutes, Epherus reaches above his head and flips a series of switches. Then, he unbuckles his harness and stands, stretching as he turns to Griz.

"Nice job," he says. "You didn't kill us."

"I thought about it, but my mate's onboard," Griz replies.

At the mention of the word *mate*, Epherus looks at me and

then at Bruce, and starts to chuckle again. Dammit. This guy is a trouble maker. A quick change of topic is in order.

"So, how did you fly this thing to Kerberos all by yourself?" I ask him.

"This ship pretty much flies itself," he says, his amusement abating. "I can do it alone, but it's easier with a co-pilot."

With that, Griz unbuckles himself and heads toward me while Epherus walks to the back of the room and monkeys around with some gadgets on the wall.

"It's safe to get up and move around now," Griz tells us as he frees me from my harness.

Bruce moves to unfasten his own harness, but struggles with all the complex buckles. Griz watches him for a moment and then finally leans over to help once it's clear that Bruce is overwhelmed.

"Hands off, alien," Bruce snaps as he slaps Griz's hand away. "All this extraterrestrial technology is enough to drive a man daft."

"Pop," I say softly, using my daddy's little girl voice that he can never resist. "Let Griz help you."

He growls at the harness one last time and then throws his hands in the air. "Fine. But don't be groping me."

Epherus chuckles from the rear.

Once Bruce is clear of his harness, we all stand up and stretch, enjoying our newfound freedom. Epherus jabs at one last button and then strolls toward the exit.

"Follow me, and I'll show you around. The ship has extra quarters if anyone wants to lie down or . . . ." He smirks at me and Griz, and I cringe, praying he won't go there. " . . . whatever."

Bruce mumbles something unintelligible, and Epherus chuckles again.

"I expect to catch up with the slave ship in approximately seven to eight hours. Make sure you're back on the bridge before then, or I'll leave your ass behind," he tells Griz.

I feel my mate tense, and I squeeze his hand, hoping to calm him down and avert any trouble. Why does Epherus have to be such a dickhead?

Hoping to lighten the tension, I throw out the first thing that comes to mind. "Well, I don't know about everyone else, but I'm starving again. Do you have any food?"

Bruce goggles at me, his jaw falling open, and Griz gives me a pleased, smug smile. For what, I have no idea.

"You just ate a seven-course meal big enough to fill up a whole crew of them blue fellas," he says, waving at Epherus. "How can you be hungry again already?"

"I don't know, but I'm famished. I can't help it," I reply, my face flaming with embarrassment.

It's Griz's turn to chuckle now, and I give him a what-the-hell look. His eyes sparkle in reply.

"This way," Epherus says. "I'll show you to the galley. I have reconstituted and field MREs. Take your pick."

Griz's face turns sour, but I just shrug. I don't care what it is, so long as it's edible. I'll inhale it at this point.

"Galley's there," Epherus tells Griz as he points to a small kitchenette. "I'm going to go catch a few winks if you can handle feeding your *mate*." He glances at Bruce and starts chuckling again.

"I think I can handle that," Griz replies coolly.

"When you're done, he can take the first room on the right," he says, waving toward Bruce. "You two . . ." he waves at me and Griz, but looks at Bruce, obviously trying to get a rise out of him. " . . . can have the second room."

I hear a low growl coming from Bruce's direction, and Epherus laughs all the way down the hall.

Good grief. This is going to be long, bloody trip, even before we catch up to Beahl.

# CHAPTER TWENTY-THREE

Griz

Watching my mate demolish her second bowl of reconstituted claffer stew, I can't help the smug grin that's plastered on my face. My chest swells with macki pride, the strength of my seed surprising even me. I have an overwhelming urge to brag to someone about my extraordinary accomplishment, but there's no one here to share in my joy. Certainly, not Bruce. I twist my head around to see if he's lurking anywhere nearby. Fortunately, he's wandered away for the moment. *Irritating male.*

I'll have to tell Aine when the moment is right. Just the mere thought of bearing younglings sent her into a certified panic earlier. She is still so young and innocent, but I know she'll make a fine dam. I look at her now, picturing her round with our youngling, her breasts swollen with sweet, life-giving milk, and her pretty, pink nipples tender and erect for nursing.

I reach beneath the table and adjust my cock. I wonder if I could take her here? I glance around making sure Bruce hasn't returned. *Annoying human.*

"Thanks, sweetheart." She pushes away her empty bowl and rubs her belly. "I don't know what's wrong with me. I've never eaten so much before. I swear I feel like I've already put on five pounds."

She truly has no clue, which I find baffling. Even her scent has changed. It's richer and sweeter, and totally intoxicating.

In three short cycles, our first youngling will be here. I can hardly believe it. I really should tell her, but I have much more pressing matters on my mind at the moment.

I stand, picking up her empty bowl and tossing it into the recycler. Then, I return to hover behind her, combing my fingers through her silky red tresses. The color reminds me of the beautiful sandy beaches on Tarilax and makes me ache for home.

"Perhaps you'd like to lie down for a bit and rest?"

She leans back, stretching and resting her head against my stomach. "That actually sounds tempting. I'm still tired, even though I slept at the hotel."

"Not nearly enough. Come on," I tell her, helping her from the chair. "We have plenty of time before we catch up with Beahl."

And, I plan to enjoy every click of it.

I force myself not to run as I lead my mate down the hallway to the ship's cabins. Tiptoeing past the room that Epherus singled out for Bruce, I stop at the one on the other side, pulling her through the door quickly and closing it as quietly as I can.

I turn around to find her smiling, her brow arched, and a knowing look on her face.

"Don't worry. He's sleeping," she says. "It would take an explosion to wake him up right now."

Well, that's a relief. I take a step inside, pausing for a long click to study this lovely, beguiling female, my mate. I can hardly believe that she's mine, my appreciation reflected in the goofy smile on my face and the rock-hard erection in my pants as I allow my gaze to cruise over her tempting curves.

"What?" she asks shyly, peeking at me from under her long ruby lashes.

"You are so beautiful, amavi." It's true. Other femkis pale in comparison. "Take off your clothes and lie down on the bed. I want to pleasure you."

She hesitates only a click before pulling the Helkon thermal shirt over her head and smoothing it neatly across the back of a chair. Her ample breasts and rosy nipples capture my attention right away, jiggling and swaying as she kicks off her boots and tugs down her pants. Pants that have taunted me for hours the way they form and hug the generous curve of her hips, the soft round globes of her ass. A slight blush creeps across her cheeks as she crawls to the middle of the bed and lies down, her eyes fastened to me.

I break my own speed-stripping record, tugging and flinging garments everywhere as my cock dances with anticipation. Then, I stalk slowly toward my mate and watch as her eyes flash, their coy innocence now replaced with raw heat and naked desire that makes me ache to sink into her. But first, her pleasure.

I prowl up the bottom of the bed, resting between her legs as I place a pillow beneath her hips and force her legs to open wide. The angle gives me a perfect view of her already juicy pussy and her tight little bottom hole.

"Wha . . . What are you doing?" she asks anxiously.

"Shh," I whisper, leaning over and tracing my finger slowly down her collarbone to her breast and pressing her pebbled nipple like a button. I catch it between my teeth, giving it a rough nip.

"Oh!" she squeaks, melting into the bed and whimpering as I slowly circle my tongue, suckling while I knead the other.

"Griz," she pants, thrusting her hips at the air and trying to press against me.

I moan a response, intentionally ignoring her sweet little core until I'm sure she's wild with need.

I move to her other nipple and give it the same attention, sucking it hard as I run my hand across the barely perceptible swell of her stomach and back up to massage her other breast.

"Griz, please," she whines, writhing and bucking beneath me. She's ready.

I sit up, dragging my fingers down her stomach to rest in the beautiful, red curls on her mound. She flexes, bucking her hips off the bed and trying to get my fingers where she needs them most.

"What is it, sweetness?" I tease, sweetly tormenting her and enjoying the sight of her heavy lids and the lusty flush on her cheeks. Her eyes blaze with desire. "Do you want me to pleasure you here?" I ask, finally dipping my finger between her folds and massaging her nub with her juices.

She moans, too far gone to make any words, but I stop before she comes, my hearts swelling at the sight of her little pout. Smiling, I move my fingers again, circling her little nub and massaging.

"Like this?"

"Yes," she pants, shifting her hips and murmuring raspy sounds of encouragement.

Shiest! My angel is soaking wet. Leaning over, my lips greet her pussy with a gentle kiss as I slide a finger inside her. She shrieks, straining her hips and swallowing my digit.

"Oh!" she cries, winding her fingers into my hair.

Taking her bud between my lips, I suck on it lightly, grazing it with my fang and flicking my tongue while I pump my finger in and out of her slit.

She screams so loud, I worry she might wake up Bruce. But then, all thoughts fly out of my head as her pussy begins to spasm and clench around my finger, her hips bucking like a wild claffer. I groan and squeeze my cock, trying to force back the flood of seed threatening to escape as I lap at her juices, bringing her gently back down.

"Griz," she pants, looking at me through dazed eyes.

She is so frizzucking beautiful like this, a sated smile on her face, and her bright, wild mane spread around her like a fiery halo.

"One more time." I smile, ignoring her protest as I lean over and plunge my tongue into her slit again.

"Griz, no!" She tries to press her thighs together. "I can't."

"You can," I argue, firmly spreading her thighs back open and holding them there. "For me, you will."

With a sigh, she opens her legs, relaxing into me as I lick and lap at her delicious folds, coaxing her back into a frenzy. Within clicks, she is writhing and pleading again. I press two fingers inside her this time, curling and gliding them in and out as I suckle her swollen bud.

She shatters again so sweetly, keening and screaming my name as she claws at the sheets, and I can't take anymore. I flip her onto her stomach before she has a chance to recover. Lifting her beautiful ass high in the air, I plunge inside her with a single thrust, nearly seizing from the sharp stab of pleasure. She cries out, her tight inner channel rippling around my cock and stealing the breath from my lungs. I groan as she tries to milk me.

Gritting my teeth until they nearly crack, I freeze, trying to wait for her contractions to pass, but they just don't stop. Her orgasm is never-ending. Beads of sweat gather on my forehead, and my body quakes, balanced precariously on the edge. Finally, the soul-sucking spasms begin to ebb, and I can breathe again. I need to take this very slow.

Aine pants, swallowing huge gulps of air as she lies in a limp heap, her face sweaty and pressed flat against the sheets. The position lifts her bottom even higher in the air, giving me a perfect view of our joining while I try to calm myself. My breath finally begins to steady, and I stroke the sweet, plump orbs of her ass laid open before me like a delicacy. I just can't help myself. The tiny little rosebud between her cheeks calls to me, beckoning my fingers like some dark treasure. I brush my thumb against it, then insert the barest tip of my finger.

Suddenly, the air inside the room shifts, charging with an energy so erotic that it crackles and sizzles against my skin. My mate's shrill screams crack through the silence like a plasma blast. Her back arched and her head flung back in ecstasy, she splinters violently all around me. Her entire body begins to spasm and contract all over again, her pussy clenching my cock so hard, my vision blurs and the veins in my neck threaten to burst from the strain.

A mighty bellow rips from my lungs, and I rut against her like a wild beast, plunging into her until I explode. My climax rips through me like Tarilean twister, wracking my body with such intense pleasure, it damn near borders pain.

Spent, my muscles trembling with aftershocks, I collapse on the bed beside my mate to catch my breath. So much for a nice, slow frizzuck. It's never going to happen with her. The thought is irritating. So, why am I smiling, then?

I twist my head to check on my immobile amavi, surprised to discover that she is already fast asleep, or passed out. With a chuckle, I jerk the sheets over us and pull her against my chest. She feels so good, a perfect fit as I spoon my body around her. Closing my eyes as I nuzzle her mane, enveloped by her sweet scent, I feel myself begin to drift.

# CHAPTER TWENTY-FOUR

Aine

I jackknife awake, gasping and my heart pounding like a bass drum against my chest. The blaring siren overhead brings back unpleasant memories of our recent escape from the slave ship, and my pulse throbs in time with each new wail.

Gris is half-dressed, his face taut and his body tense as he steps into his boots and makes his way back over to the bed.

"What is it? What's happening?"

He bends over, planting a chaste kiss on my lips. "I don't know. Get dressed and meet me on the bridge. I'm going to go find out."

I nod anxiously, tossing the sheet aside and scrambling around for my clothes. Griz leaves as I'm jumping into my panties, frantically reaching for the next article of clothing. I pull my shirt over my head and tug it over my stomach, the smart fabric molding around me and supporting me better than any sports bra ever could. I spy my pants on the floor and kick them in the air with a flick of my ankle, snatching them and hopping around while I try to lasso my foot.

Once I finally get them on, I have to suck in my breath to fasten them. This is ridiculous. I'll have to check with Griz later and see what they put in their food. I'd bet my new boots they're chocked so full of calories, I'll end up having to eat space carrots for the rest of my life.

I tear out the door as soon as I get my boots on, suddenly

wishing I'd taken the time to at least wash my face and finger-comb my hair. But I guess it doesn't matter if we're all about to die. I'm still trying to master walking fast and tying on my thigh holster at the same time when I emerge onto the bridge. The scene in front of me is chaotic, to say the least, and I stand there blinking dumbly as I try to absorb the situation.

"Turn off that frizzucking alarm," Griz growls as he dances around the far end of the console, his fingers flying over a key pad entering God-only-knows-what.

Epherus reaches quickly, but calmly, over his head and flicks a single switch. Thankfully, the sirens cease. Now, if only the ringing in my ears would stop.

A bright burst of light suddenly explodes at the right front side of the window, and I feel a tremor at my feet slowly vibrating up my legs. What the hell was that? As the light fades, I see the dark, hulking shape of a behemoth ship ahead in the distance. Another white-hot pulse rockets from the rear of the vessel, too fast for my eyes to follow, but the subsequent effulgent explosion and jarring jolts beneath my boots leaves no doubt. We're under fire.

"Damage?" Epherus looks at Griz, unflustered and unimpressed.

Griz punches some buttons on the other console and frowns at the screen. "Minimal. Shields holding at ninety-three percent."

"What the feck is going on here?" Bruce bursts into the room, his clothes crumpled, his hair an unruly mess of tangles sticking up in every direction.

Griz spins around, noticing me for the first time. "Aine."

"Strap in, humans," Epherus says without a backward glance. "The ride's about to get bumpy."

I look at Bruce, waving at him to follow me to the chairs.

"They're firing at us," I explain.

Then, as if to prove my point, another explosion fills the

front window, and the floor shimmies angrily, harder than the last time. I stagger toward the seats, my legs feeling all noodly, like I'm running in a funhouse at the fair.

"That one was a direct hit," Griz informs Epherus.

"Those bloody scunners," Bruce grumbles. "I ain't curling up in a little ball and trembling like some dainty little wallflower. I'm going out fighting," he shouts.

"We can't return fire," Griz replies as he taps wildly on the console again. "We're down to seventy-two, and there's an asteroid field straight ahead," he tells Epherus.

"I'm pulling back." Epherus mumbles a curse as he reaches over and tugs on a shiny, grey lever that looks like something I'd see in an airplane cockpit. I feel the ship lurch, and my butt lifts up out of my seat while my shaky hands work on fastening the frustrating buckles.

Bruce staggers forward, grabbing hold of the back of Griz's seat to steady himself.

"What do you mean, we can't fire back?" he asks incredulously.

"Beahl's ship is full of innocent femkis," Griz snaps. "You'd have us blow them up?"

"My sister's onboard that ship," Epherus snarls threateningly, as if Griz was suggesting that we should.

"I thought you was going to beam yourself over there or some such havers?" Bruce argues.

"We can't," Griz tells him, excitedly twirling knobs and spinning dials. "We can't get close enough."

Suddenly, a loud boom rocks the entire ship, rattling my teeth and jarring my bones. I watch with horrible fascination as Bruce sails past me and lands on his face on the other side of the room. Lights flicker and dim, and a red glow floods the bridge as brand new sirens begin to wail. I think my eardrums are bleeding.

Did they hit us?

"Bruce!" I shout, trying to unfasten the buckles I just got fastened.

"I'm alright, lass" he replies, rising to his forearms and shaking his head. "Stay where you are."

For the first time, I see Epherus in what might be described as a panic, flicking off his harness and leaping from his chair.

"Kill the engines," he yells over his shoulder at Griz.

Griz doesn't reply, but I can see an entire monologue written on his face, one that only ends in tragedy.

We're going to die.

Epherus storms toward the back of the room, scooping up Bruce as he passes, almost as an afterthought, and depositing him in front of a little black screen on the wall.

"Watch this and don't move," he growls. "Tell me if it falls below fourteen salibytes."

What the fuck is a salibyte?

I don't have time to ask as Epherus flies back to the front of the ship and slaps on a headset, his fingers moving to a small panel where he begins punching in numbers and twirling knobs.

"Assassin Four to Mera's Arc," he says.

He depresses a button in the middle of the panel, and a static-y crackle fills the air. Ripping the headset off, he tosses it onto the console and races across the room to a flashing red light on the wall.

"Come in, Mera's Arc," he shouts in his deep, baritone voice that makes me shiver. Still not in a good way. "This is Assassin Four," he says, flipping open a panel next to the red light.

"Eff!" A smooth, husky voice cuts through the static. "We thought you were dead."

"Not yet," Epherus scoffs. "Zeph, I need a rendez-vous and take-over on a Class D Quantum Cargo Cruiser at the following coordinates."

He rattles off a series of coordinates as his hands disappear into a panel on the wall, fidgeting with whatever's inside until a spray of sparks hits him right in the face.

"Godsdammit," he says, dragging his big paw over his face, and then continuing on with the coordinates.

"What the hell are you doing?" I shriek at Epherus.

"We're on fire," he replies like it's no big deal.

The ship's going to explode, and we're all going to be burned to space ash. No biggie.

"Did you get those coordinates, Zeph?"

"Let me repeat," the voice on speaker says, launching into the long string of numbers again.

"Affirmative," Epherus replies, then, seemingly frustrated, he stabs his whole hand into the panel and jerks out a handful of wires.

The alarms suddenly stop, and the red glow is replaced with dim, flickering lights.

"Do not . . . I repeat . . . Do not fire on that ship, Zeph. There's innocent civilians onboard. Take control, detain the ship and its occupants, and hold until I get there."

"Since when do you care about innocent civilians," the voice laughs.

"Just secure the ship and its contents until I get there," he says, apparently not as amused by the guy's snarky comment.

"Understood. I'll com you as soon as we're there."

"Out," Epherus says, striding back to the console and flicking a single switch. Calm returns to his movements as he looks back at Bruce. "What are we sitting at?"

"We're down to seventeen salibytes," Bruce replies.

"Whatever you did, the fire's out in Section Seven," Griz says, spinning his chair around to face us.

Epherus grumbles something in response, then retakes his seat in the front.

"That's the good news. There's also a hull breach in

Compartment Five, but I've sealed it off." Griz reports.

"And, the bad news?" Epherus pounds a fist against a panel on the dashboard, and it pops open.

"Well, the breach is the least of our worries right now. It looks like the fire has affected the ship's electrical system, and we've lost the carbitrister and the shields."

"Is that all?" Epherus scoffs sarcastically, his fingers busy twining more wires in the panel.

"Nope. The hyperdrive is shot, too." Griz spins around in his chair and crosses his arms, as if his work here is now done.

"Life support systems?"

"Holding," Griz cuts his eyes to me, the relief reflected in them obvious even as his voice maintains a cold, detached tone.

"What does all that mean?" I ask him.

"Basically, we're floating around like a Haepler leaf on the wind," he explains. "And, our shields are down because of the fire. If we get hit by another pulse or even a small piece of that asteroid before they come back up, we're effectively toast."

# Chapter Twenty-five

Aine

M y eyes dart behind him to the window, searching for a sign of Beahl's ship or anything larger than a pebble that might be drifting our way. I may not have understood everything he said, like what a carbo-rooster is, but I know we're in a bad spot. I chew on my lip as my mind flips through potential disaster scenarios.

Griz gets up and walks over to me, sitting down in the empty chair beside me and taking my hand in his.

"It'll be alright, sweetling," he says, pressing a kiss to the back of my hand.

Will it? I'm not so sure. Then, a thought hits me, and I shout, "Bruce!"

"Aye, lass?"

"No. I wasn't calling—" I pause, hoping what I'm about to say doesn't sound too stupid. I know a spaceship is not a house or an Earth construction, but surely, electricity works the same everywhere? "You said the fire was electrical. Right?"

"Yes," Griz nods, and then, his face lights with understanding. "Bruce can fix it," he says, his voice filling with hope.

"Aye. Possibly." Bruce frowns, his eyes glued to the wall panel he's in charge of monitoring. "If I had the right tools, and if it's not too . . . alien."

I look at Epherus to gauge his reaction, disappointed as he appears unmoved by our discussion.

"Oh, and Ephipus," he says, intentionally mispronouncing Epherus' name. "We're still at seventeen of those salibyte things."

Griz sniggers, possibly catching on to Bruce's name game, and leans in to give me a little kiss on my lips, one that I take full advantage of. Maybe it's the relief that we're all still alive, or the simple fact that he's just plain fucking tasty. Whatever the reason, I melt into him, my tongue sneaking between his lips and savoring him until I feel my underwear growing damp. I don't stop until I hear Bruce cough and Epherus clear his throat uncomfortably. I catch Griz's bottom lip between my teeth as I pull back, promising more to come, and leave him rumbling.

"You think he can actually fix the shields and the carbitrister?" Epherus jerks his head toward Bruce and looks at us doubtfully.

"It's certainly worth a try," Griz replies. "He was able to dismantle the remote to our slave implants."

"I'll need tools," Bruce informs them.

Epherus still doesn't look convinced.

"I guess he can't break it any worse," he finally reasons. Getting up from his chair, he sighs and jerks his chin toward Bruce. "Follow me, human."

"What about these salad-byte thingies?" he asks, once again purposely slaughtering the word. It's an old joke he's used on me for years in a determined attempt to drive me insane. Epherus doesn't appear to have much of a sense of humor, though.

"Salibytes," he growls.

"Whatever," Bruce taunts. "Don't I need to watch them? I thought we were going to blow up or die horribly with our skin peeling off if it falls below the fourteen mark?"

"If it's still hovering around the seventeen SSI mark, we're fine."

Bruce squints and bobs his neck forward, his nose nearly touching the plate. "Yep. Still seventeen."

"Then, come with me," Epherus says as he storms off the bridge.

Griz and I trail behind as I struggle to keep up with Epherus' brisk pace through the many winding passages. Everything goes smoothly until we run smack into a solid wall.

"What the Haelic?" Epherus runs his hands over the wall looking for a doorway or some other kind of entry.

"That's Compartment Five," Griz says, huffing as he drags his fingers through his hair. "There's no way in. It's sealed."

"Shiest!" Epherus shouts and punches the wall.

I flinch, but quickly decide I'm glad he took out his anger on the wall, and not on Griz or Bruce. Or me, either, for that matter. There's a huge dent where he smacked it.

"Can't we get around it?" It's probably a dumb question, but someone's got to ask it.

"Depends," Griz says. "Where's engineering?"

Epherus turns around, a scowl etched into his stony face. "Compartment Five."

Agitated, Griz combs his fingers through his hair, muttering curses beneath his breath.

"Is there no other access to the electrical? If we have to, I can drill into the wall or crawl up in the ceiling," Bruce offers.

Epherus sighs. "Maybe, but the tools you'd need for that are in there," he says, tipping his head toward the big metal wall in front of us. He scratches his head and looks at Bruce. "However, the main circuitry is actually over there on the port side."

"Now we're talking, Big Guy. Can we get to it without having to go in there?" Bruce jerks his thumb toward the wall in front of us.

"Yeah. It's actually on the outside of the ship." Epherus

shrugs.

"The feck, you say," Bruce shakes his head and backs away from Epherus. "You're a flaming radge if you think I'm going out there."

"Relax. I'll go, and you can walk me through it. Unless . . . ." His face lights with an idea, and he pushes past us, stomping back down the hall.

We scramble to keep up, turning down a different passageway on our left this time. Finally, we land in an expansive room with two covered pod-looking things, some lockers and about a half dozen spacesuits hanging on hooks against one wall. The other wall is just one big hatch, the only thing standing between us and the vast emptiness of space. The thought makes me shudder.

"Why can't we just take those?" I ask, waving toward the smaller pods. As long as I'm asking stupid questions, I may as well continue the trend.

"They aren't made for long-range travel," Epherus explains. "There's nowhere close enough for us to land. But, if it comes down to it and we have to abandon ship, I'll fire off another com, and we'll use the pods, anyway. I'm just not quite ready to write her off yet."

I breathe a sigh of relief. At least, we have an emergency backup plan.

"In the meantime, I totally forgot about this," Epherus says excitedly as he scoops one of the suits off a hook and tosses it on top of a pod so it's out of the way. "There."

He points to a small electrical panel that appears on the wall behind where the suit hung moments before.

"Step aside." Bruce stalks forward as if he's advancing on a murder scene. Squeezing in front of Epherus, he pries open the panel.

"Hm," he muses as he scratches his chin and studies the box. Without a word, he reaches out and flips a series of switches simultaneously. Sparks fly everywhere, and the box sizzles as the ship lets out an eerie death moan.

Epherus narrows his eyes at an unfazed Bruce, his fists opening and closing, and I'm suddenly afraid for Bruce's continued well-being.

"What just happened?" I ask Bruce as I step in between him and Epherus.

"The mainframe transformer is blown," he says calmly, twisting around to look at Griz. "Give me your knife, alien."

Griz's eyes go wide as he seems to consider the consequences of arming Bruce with a sharp instrument. He glances at me for approval, and I give him a nod. With a shrug, Griz digs out a small pocket knife and tosses it to Bruce. Snatching it out of the air, Bruce turns around and begins tinkering with the box again.

"What are you doing now?" Epherus asks, apparently deciding to micro-manage the project.

"Stripping these wires," Bruce replies brusquely as he scrapes the knife up and down several of the wires, peeling back the outer skins. "Aine, give me some light."

I pat my pockets in hopes a flashlight might magically appear. But, nope. No such luck. Fortunately, Epherus strides over to a locker in the corner and pulls out something that looks like an eight-ball with a handle. He rubs his hand across the front, and the whole thing begins to glow. Voila! Magic eight-ball.

He hands the glowing device to me, and I hold it strategically over the box while Bruce's fingers are busy twisting and curling together various wires. When he's done, he frowns at it, then turns around to survey the room.

"What are you looking for?" I ask, holding up the glow-ball to cast more light around the room.

"Nothing," he finally says as he sits down on the floor and begins to cut out little chunks of his boot heel. When he's done, he carves a hollow space in the middle of the chunks and uses them to cap the freshly connected wires.

After a few minutes of solemn silence, Bruce slaps the panel shut and turns around. "You'll still have to go outside to replace the fuses on the main transformer. But, once you do that and flip the breakers back on, it should work."

Epherus stares wordlessly at Bruce, the silence stretching so long, it starts to get a little weird.

"You don't have any new fuses, do you?" Bruce finally says.

"Yes, I do," Epherus snaps defensively.

"Okay. Where are they?"

"In Compartment Five," Epherus admits sheepishly.

"Well, shite." Bruce huffs and begins to scratch his chin again contemplatively. With a shrug, he looks at Epherus. "Suit me up."

What?

"No. Bruce, you're not going out there," I inform him.

"He canna do what needs to be done, Aine. I have to do it."

"Bullshit!" I argue. "Just what is it that no one else can seem to do except you?"

"First of all, mind your language and your tone, lassie. Now, when I first met your mum, I had this old fifty-seven Chevy that was up on blocks more than it was on the road," he says, smiling nostalgically. "I couldn't afford all the parts I needed back then, so I used to rig up old fuses by wrapping them in tin foil. It's an old trick, but it works. If you do it just right."

How can I argue with that?

"Fine, but I'm going with you."

"No!" Bruce and Griz shout at the same time, confusing me so that I don't know who to scowl at.

"Look, it's too dangerous to go out there by yourself. If anything happens, you need backup. I'm coming," I insist, nearly stomping my foot.

Bruce sighs in defeat. "Fine."

"No! Not with the youngling!" Griz suddenly shouts, grabbing my arm and pulling me to him.

"What?" Bruce and I shout at the same time, turning to stare at him while Epherus' loud guffaws echo like gunshots throughout the room.

There is something seriously wrong with that guy.

"I . . . Uh . . ." Griz's deer-in-the-headlights look is kind of cute. His eyes finally settle on Bruce in desperation, and he makes a gallant effort to change the topic by lashing out at him. "This is exactly what I was talking about. You've just let her take charge and do whatever she wants, without any discipline at all."

I gawk at him like he's crazy, and when his words finally sink in, I square my shoulders and shirk his hand off my arm.

"What. The. Fuck. Are you saying?"

# Chapter Twenty-six

Griz

How the Haelic am I going to get out of this one? I panicked and said the first thought that popped into my head, and, as usual, it was the wrong one. Now, my mate looks like a deranged pixie, and she's more determined than ever to take a romp in space.

"I didn't mean it that way, amavi," I whimper.

"I'm not sure exactly how many different ways that could have been meant," she snaps.

"I only care for your safety, my love."

"Yeah? I care about my pop's safety," she says, her little nostrils flaring. "I'm going with him."

Panic squeezes my throat again. "You can't put the youngling in that kind of danger!"

Well, frizzuck.

Aine and Bruce stare at me as if I've just sprouted horns like Epherus. Speaking of Epherus, that idiot is laughing again. Bent over, holding his sides, cackling like a hyenstra.

If I leaned over and punched him in the nuts, I wonder if he'd stop?

"What are you talking about, Griz?"

My poor mate looks on the verge of implosion now. This is not how I envisioned telling her.

"I will go with him," I say in hopes of heading off that topic.

"Oh, no, you don't. That's the second time you've

mentioned 'youngling.' Tell me what you're talking about," she says, shaking her head.

Briefly, I consider grabbing her and kissing her really hard as a distraction tactic, but I don't think it will work this time.

"Aine, amavi. You are ripe with my seed. You carry our youngling. I cannot let you go spacewalking."

"Ripe with your seed?" she repeats. "Carrying our—"

Suddenly, she stops, her face turning a greenish color, and she claps a hand over her mouth. Her stomach heaves, and she races to the other side of the room, retching loudly behind one of the escape pods. Bruce and I glare at each other as the sound of her heaving fills the air.

"What in the seven hells have you done now, alien?" Bruce takes a threatening step toward me.

"Calm down," I tell him. "Aine is my mate."

He snarls and steps over Epherus, who's rolling around on the floor laughing.

"Bruce, this is actually wonderful news," I tell him, taking a step back. "You're going to be a grandsire," I shout over my shoulder as I turn around and bolt.

Several clicks later, after Bruce wore himself out chasing me around the ship, and once I was sure he wasn't going to try and kill me again, we re-gathered by the pods.

"You're sure this will work?" Aine asks Bruce nervously, her face still a little pale. "You know what you're doing?"

"Your mum dinnae marry me fur my money or my good looks, lass," Bruce replies as Epherus fastens the last buckle on his suit. He gives her a wink, and then scowls at me.

"I won't let him out of my sight," I assure her, trying to get back into her good graces.

She glances over her shoulder and gives me a threatening look, as if I conspired with my seed to impregnate her.

I shrink back a step, figuring it might be a good idea to give her some room right now. Perhaps it's actually good that I'm about to jet into space. Once my helmet is secured, I give Epherus a nod, and he secures Bruce's helmet. We move toward the hatch together, and I turn to Epherus one last time.

"Take care of her," I tell him. Not because I don't expect to come back, but you never know. Spacewalking is always dangerous.

Epherus tips his chin in understanding as he takes Aine by the arm and leads her to the door.

"What? Why'd he say that?" she asks Epherus, before calling back over her shoulder to me. "Why'd you say that?"

I watch as my mate locks her legs stubbornly and turns around to face me and Bruce one more time, her eyes flitting back and forth between the two of us.

"I *will* see you both back here in a few minutes," she says in her haughty tone, her anger all but forgotten.

"Of course you will." I give her the brightest smile I can muster as the door slides shut between us.

"Ready?" I ask Bruce as I fasten the leads to our belts and twist the hatch release.

"As I'll ever be," he replies.

The air sucks out of the room with a whoosh as I slide open the external hatch. I hang on to the wall rail with one hand and to Bruce with the other until the pressure stabilizes. Then, I loosen our leads and kick off the side of the ship, pulling Bruce behind me.

I still think it was the best decision not to teach Bruce how to use the suit's thrusters. It's safer to just keep him tied to me. Knowing him, he'd thrust himself into a black hole, and we'd never be able to find him.

So, with several short, controlled thrusts, we make it over to the ship's main transformer in good time. I tug him to me and hold him steady as he enters the code to the transformer panel that Epherus provided. I breathe a sigh of relief when the panel hisses open.

"Light," he snaps as if he's about to perform a delicate brain surgery.

Sniggering, I pull the torch from my belt and activate it, holding it between him and the transformer box. He begins fingering several of the obviously burned out fuses and then plucks one out, twisting it in the foil that we cut from the pod tarps before working it carefully back into place. I'm actually impressed by his stealth and skill, and everything seems to be going smoothly until we get to the last fuse.

"Feck!" he shouts, and I watch in horror as the tiny fuse tumbles away from his hand toward the dark void of outer space.

I leap, trying to snag it before it's out of reach, but I'm tugged backward by the lead just as my fingertips graze the tip.

"Shiest!"

"What is it? What's happened?" Epherus' voice fills my helmet, but I've no time to explain.

"Bruce, hang on to the ship, and don't let go," I tell him as I unfasten the lead and kick off.

I keep my eyes locked onto the minuscule fuse so I don't lose it. I'd never be able to find it again. The further away from the ship I float, the darker and quieter it becomes, and then, I lose the short-range com built into my suit. After that, the only sound I can hear is myself breathing. Discomfiting against the looming backdrop of space.

One more thrust . . . I force myself not to take a wild grab at it, instead slowly and carefully reaching out to palm it into my gloved hand.

"Got it!" I say victoriously, but no one can hear me. I turn around to make my way back, and my stomach fills with dread.

Frizzuck. The ship looks like a little spec in the distance.

How the Haelic did I get so far away? I cut my eyes to the air gauge on the right side of my helmet shield, praying I have enough to get back. It will be close.

With tiny, measured thrusts, I slowly make my way back, turning off my com halfway there so I don't have to hear any more of Bruce's angry threats or curses from Epherus. Emptying my tank, I thrust one last time, attaching myself to the side of the ship like a hungry parasite.

"Don't do that again," Bruce growls at me.

"You don't do that again," I snarl back.

He glares at me for a moment, and then smiles. "Good job, alien."

Happier than I thought I'd be after receiving praise from my sire-in-law, I watch as he takes the wayward fuse from my hand and wraps it in the foil. I hold my breath until he pops it into place with the others.

"Now. Cross your fingers," he says.

Cross my fingers? How will that help? I don't question him — I just do my best to cross them inside the clumsy gloves of my suit.

Suddenly, Bruce flicks the main switches all at once, and I hear the comforting rumble and whir of the engines kick back on. Lights flicker and engage, illuminating the ship.

"You did it!" I shout, more in disbelief than anything else.

"Of course I did," he replies with a roll of his eyes. "Now, let's get the feck out of here. All this space gives me the willies."

My thrusters empty, we're forced to crawl across the ship like spiders all the way back to the hatch. Finally, I pull myself inside, yanking Bruce in behind me and muscling the hatch closed again. My ears pop like ruptured balloons as pressure returns to the room, but it's a small price to pay to be back onboard the ship.

Reaching out, I unfasten Bruce's helmet first and then start to work on my own as the inside door slides open, and Aine races through. She slams into me, nearly knocking me off my feet.

"You scared the shit out of me," she cries.

I drop my helmet and wrap my arms around my hysterical mate, kissing her hair and comforting her as her shoulders shake against me. I glance over at Bruce who eyes us uncomfortably, and offers no assistance with consoling Aine.

"I'm sorry, amavi. All is well, and I'm back," I whisper to her. "Now, stop leaking."

This makes her snort a giggle, which I find strangely attractive. Finally, she releases me, wiping her cheeks with the back of her hand and then punching me in the chest. She is such a confusing femki sometimes.

Suddenly, she seems to remember that her sire made it back, as well.

"Bruce," she sighs, and throws her hands around his neck.

"It's okay, lass," he says, patting her back awkwardly.

"Good job," Epherus announces as he joins the reunion, jerking his chin at me. "You, too, human."

"Thanks," Bruce says, seeming relieved when Aine finally releases him. He clears his throat and pats her on the head, before turning around to unsuit.

"Are the shields back up?" I ask, hoping to get the Haelic out of here.

Epherus nods as he hangs my spent suit back on its hook. "We have shields, and I think we can make it to the next port for repairs. We'll have to take it easy, though, and not put too much stress on the carbitrister. If it burns out, we're really in trouble. Of course, we also can't use the hyperdrive."

"What's the next port?" I ask, snaking my arm around my mate and pulling her close to my side. "And, how long will it take us to get there without a hyperdrive?"

"We're in the Fosterus galaxy," he replies. "The next port

is located on Gysteros, and without the hyperdrive, it's going to take approximately five Earth days to get there. If we're lucky."

"When will your team make the rendez-vous with Beahl's ship?"

"Tomorrow," he says, taking Bruce's suit and hanging it next to mine. "Depending on how long it takes to complete the repairs, it could be a cycle or more before we get there. I can't leave port again without access to the engine room, and there's no telling what the damage looks like in there."

"What does all that mean?" my mate asks me.

"It means that we won't be rendez-vous-ing with Epherus' team as we'd originally planned. We'll have to come up with a Plan B."

"Come, and let's get started figuring out what Plan B is," Epherus says. "We just need to run a quick systems check first."

My hopes for killing Beahl all but shrivel to dust. I nod at Epherus and lead Aine back toward the bridge. After strapping her safely back in, I return to my chair at the console and kickoff the systems checks.

"Come in, Mera's Arc." I hear Epherus behind me trying to hail his team. "This is Assassin Four. Come in."

"We hear you, Eff." Zeph's response comes in loud and clear.

"ETA to rendez-vous?"

I pull off the results of the systems check as Zeph confirms Epherus' arrival estimate.

"I'm afraid I'll be delayed," he tells Zeph. "Do what you have to do, but make sure you take the lizard Beahl alive. Save him for me until I get there."

"He's mine!" my mate suddenly shouts, and I spin around in my chair, barely avoiding whiplash.

She turns her head slowly, meeting every pair of eyes in

the room. "I want to be the one to kill him."

More than ever, the memory of my mate retching over her toilet in her cell haunts me. What did he do to her?

"We'll see," Epherus finally says as Zeph chuckles into the overhead.

"Popular guy," Zeph replies.

"I need you to confirm the identity of one Lla'anya Zinto, too. She'll be held in the prisoner cells," Epherus says, and the quiet on the other end of the com suggests Zeph knows exactly who that is.

"You got it," Zeph finally replies, all traces of humor gone from his voice. "I'll com you as soon as it's done."

Epherus tosses his headset onto the console and strides over to the chair next to me. "Status?"

"We're good to go," I tell him. "I just sent you the coordinates."

"Settle in, folks. We're headed to Gysteros."

# Chapter Twenty-seven

Aine

Yawning, I stretch and roll over, smiling as I recall the ceremony. The month we spent on Gysteros afterward is still fresh in my memory. Tarileans may not do honeymoons, but that's how I'll always think of our time there. Our honeymoon. And Griz made sure it was perfect, even if my father had to tag along.

My Griz is so sweet. I reach out and stroke his thick, golden hair as he sleeps, and I'm rewarded with a growl as he reaches out and drags me to him. I giggle, but the hard edges of his seriously cut body and the stiff cock poking me in my big, pregnant belly are anything but funny.

"Mm," I moan, taking my time as I smooth my fingers down the ropey muscles of his arm. There's no rush. We have the rest of our lives to wake up like this.

Only a couple of months ago, if someone would have told me that I'd be married in space with a child on the way, I would have called them nuts. Hell, if they'd told me I'd be married period, I would have called them nuts. But, I was. I did. And I'm blissfully happy.

Maybe Griz couldn't find a priest or a preacher, but the shaman who was waiting for us when we reached the port on Gysteros still did an excellent job. My wedding was gorgeous. My dress was beautiful, the flowers were lovely, and Griz's vows warmed my heart. I swear Epherus' eyes were watering, but best of all, Bruce is happy.

199

Everything would be ideal if only Griz's mum and Epherus' sister would have been able to attend. Well, that, and if we'd been able to meet up with Zeph's ship. Unfortunately, many of the prisoners needed medical attention after our miserable escape attempt, including Celia. They couldn't afford to wait around for us. So, we planned to hook up at an alternate destination, instead.

It's probably for the best, anyway. The repairs took a lot longer than we'd hoped. Though, I really didn't mind that much. Gysteros turned out to be a tropical paradise. Every time I closed my eyes on the beach, I imagined I was on one of the Hawaiian islands, sipping Mai Tais and waiting on a luau to start. Except, there were no luaus and no Mai Tais. Not for me, anyway. Alcohol, grass skirts, and babies don't mix.

As if reading my mind, Griz reaches down and rubs my swollen tummy. I cannot believe how huge I am already. With the gestation time for Tarileans being only three months, I'm nervous as hell, but hoping that I carry a bit longer than that. The baby is half-human, after all. My thoughtful mate com'd ahead, and there's supposed to be a physician waiting for us who specializes in human hybrid deliveries. I find this hard to believe, but we'll see, I guess.

"I hope we're still on-schedule," I tell him, unable to contain my excitement. I can't wait to see my new home.

"We should arrive on Tarilax sometime after breakfast," he says with a mischievous gleam in his eye. "But, we still have plenty of time."

"Plenty of time for what?" I ask innocently, fully comprehending the weight of his words.

"For this!" He flips me over, attacking me with tickles and kisses while I shriek and buck beneath him. But truthfully, I love every second of it.

Suddenly, he stills, gazing at me like an apex predator, and I watch as his eyes grow dark. His playful smile dissolves, melting into something else, something far more menacing. He bends his head, pressing his lips to mine in a heated kiss, his touch leaving a trail of fire on my skin as his hips flex against mine.

Then, all thoughts of Gysteros, Tarilax, weddings, and babies melt away.

"Is that it?"

I stand behind Griz's seat, bouncing on the balls of my feet and pointing toward the tarmac just below where a crowd is gathered. Why so many people?

"It is." He twists around and pulls me onto his lap. "That's my cousin and his family, several of my extended relations, and some of Horok's personnel and well-wishers."

He sounds nervous so I smile and give him a chaste kiss on his cheek. "It's going to be fine. They obviously love you. Why else would they all be here?"

"I know. I just haven't seen them in so long. It feels strange. I left here two rotations ago as a king's guard on a general excursion, and now return as a slave with no honor and no dignity. It's . . . difficult."

Nuh-uh. I'm not having this.

"You're wrong," I tell him, sitting up and holding his face so he has to look me in the eye. "You're returning as a proud, brave warrior, who helped to save more than a hundred helpless girls from all across the universe. On top of that, who knows how many other men and women you saved by preventing that prick from doing it again? You're not a slave. You're a hero, Griz."

He gives me a shaky smile and kisses my forehead.

"And, most importantly, you're my beloved mate, and sire of my son," I remind him. "Don't you forget it."

He places his hand on top of my belly, rubbing over the fabric of my new dress that he bought me on our honeymoon.

One of the benefits of pregnancy, I have a whole new wardrobe.

"I would never forget that, amavi," he whispers so that only I can hear.

"You need to set her down and strap her in long enough for us to land," Epherus says, intruding on our moment.

Griz sighs, smiling as he picks me up and waltzes me to a seat next to Bruce where he deposits me gently.

"First time I've ever seen a green Aurelian," Griz says teasingly as he buckles me in. "I guess envy will do that to any macki."

"Pfft. Envy what? A nagging mate and a hover truck full of dirty diapers every day?" Epherus scoffs.

"Yeah. I can't wait." Griz smiles as he returns to his seat next to Epherus.

"Well, doona look at me," Bruce chimes in. "Aine's mum did all the diaper changing in our hoose. I wouldna ken which end to powder and which end to kiss."

This earns him a chuckle from Epherus. "Get ready. We're setting down."

I barely feel my butt cheeks lift off the seat as we finally set down on Tarilax. My heart is racing, and I'm sweating in some really weird places. I have no idea why I'm so nervous.

"We made it." I smile at Bruce, and he pats my hand affectionately.

"Nice landing," Griz says as he flips off his buckle and comes to rescue me from the halter that he just strapped me into.

"Practically lands itself," Epherus replies, turning his sharp eyes toward Bruce. "What are you going to do now, human?"

"Who? Me?" Bruce looks at him, confused.

"Yes. You. What are your plans? Are you settling down on Tarilax, too?"

"I doona ken," Bruce says, his bushy eyebrows knitting

together. "I haven't really given it much thought."

What the hell? He's thinking about leaving me? I'd never even considered the possibility. Talk about putting a damper on my excitement.

"I have need of an engineer," Epherus says. "The job is yours if you want it."

Our necks ricochet in unison as Griz and I both turn to see Bruce's reaction. He raises an eyebrow at the alien as he rubs the back of his neck.

"Can I think on it?"

"Yeah. Let's go meet your adoring fans," Epherus says, heading toward the exit.

Griz holds my hand, tugging me forward as my nerves begin eating away at my resolve. There sure are a lot of people out there.

Epherus opens the exterior door, and a gust of warm air swooshes in to greet me. The scent of flowers and freshly mowed grass floats gently on the breeze, reminding me of home. My nerves begin to relax, and I look at Griz as he squeezes my hand.

"We're home," he says.

I can barely hear myself think as we descend into the mob below. Throngs of people reach out and touch us, shouting welcomes and well wishes. I feel like royalty as Griz leads me through the cheering crowd. These sure are a lot of friendly people.

We finally stop in front of a handsome, haughty man who actually looks a lot like Griz. He's surrounded by a horde of females. Human females! A couple of them have toddlers in their arms, adorable boys, and I'm excited to think our son might have playmates. All the women are gorgeous, and it seems like each has a friendly smile for me. An older couple stands behind them, the man holding yet another toddler, a beautiful, spunky little girl with long, dark curls and rosy cheeks, and who's climbing him like a jungle gym. He certainly doesn't seem to mind, though.

"Your Majesty," Griz blurts suddenly, dropping to his knee in front of the guy who looks just like him and leaving me standing there like an idiot.

Holy shit! This is his cousin? The king? I must look freaked out, or murderous because I'm thinking about killing Griz later. At any rate, I'm rescued by a young, dark-haired woman who takes pity on me.

"You must be Aine," she says.

Grateful, I smile and shake her hand. "Yes, Aine MacTavish."

And, because I'm nervous and my filter isn't working, I start blurting. "You . . . you're human."

"Yep. Commander Cora Carter, at your service," she replies, shaking my hand enthusiastically. "I can't tell you how happy we are to have you guys here with us finally. You have no idea. My mate has missed his cousin so much, and we need more human females around here. Let me introduce you."

I look around at the swell of people, overwhelmed, and my knees almost knocking together. Thank God Griz is standing up again so I can lean against him.

"This is my mate, Horok," she tells me as she places her hand softly on his arm.

At least, she didn't say King Horok. I have no idea how to curtsy, and getting down on a knee is out of the question with my gigantic belly, so I nod slowly and hope that works. He smiles, nodding back.

"My cousin's mate is always welcome," he says as he steps forward and gives Griz a bear hug.

I try to let go of Griz's hand so he can hug the man back, but he only clenches it tighter. Secretly, I'm glad, but I try to act put out. When they get through man-patting each other, Cora continues.

"And, these three little rascals you see here are all ours. That's Hector, that's Xavian, and there's our little princess, little Felina."

As if to show off, the sweet little dumpling waves and shouts, "Fina!"

"All right, drama queen." Cora laughs, and Horok puffs out his chest proudly.

"Three?" Griz raises his brow at Horok.

"Try and top that." He smirks.

When we're through laughing, Cora picks back up on the introductions. "This is my crew, Maggie, Emily, Shauna, Lisa, and Dee, and that's our friend Nordric."

"Nice to meet you," I say, nodding to each as Griz shakes their hands. All of the women are human.

"And, these are Horok's parents, King Xavian and Queen Felina."

Damn. Why didn't I have Griz teach me to curtsy?

"It's an honor to meet you," I tell them, trying to bow without much success.

"The honor is ours, dear." King Xavian smiles graciously and then directs his attention to Griz. "Nephew. We thank the Goddess for delivering you safely. We thought you were lost to us," he says to Griz, stepping forward and wrapping him in a one-arm hug while the little girl pulls on Griz's hair.

"Thank you, Uncle," Griz replies, hugging him back, and then turning his attention to the regal woman by his side. "Aunt Felina."

"My little Griz," she says, stepping forward and pulling him down so she can kiss his cheeks. "As my mate said, you have been sorely missed, Nephew."

She pats his face lovingly, and since he doesn't cry, I take the responsibility onto myself and do it for him. Bruce steps behind me and places a supportive hand on my shoulder.

"Now, we have a surprise for you, Griz."

I watch as his aunt steps aside, revealing a beautiful older woman of stately stature, with long blonde hair and golden honey-colored eyes. Eyes that I know very well now. For the first time since we left the ship, Griz releases my hand.

"My dam," he says, almost on a breath. He rushes forward, picking the woman up and hugging her to him, burying his face in her hair.

"Oh, my Griz. My sweet little macki," she repeats over and over.

"I'm so sorry. Are you all right? Did they hurt you?" he asks when he finally sets her down.

"I'm fine. They didn't hurt me," she says. "I'm just glad to be home."

"How did you get free?"

"Horok," she says simply, looking at him over Griz's shoulder and smiling sweetly. "He and Nordric saved me."

"I'm forever in your debt," Griz tells Horok, and then bows to Nordric.

"It was nothing," Nordric replies. "Beahl's guards were more than happy to tell us where she was."

"Yeah, with a little Tarilean persuasion." Horok chuckles.

Smiling, Griz takes his mother's arm and leads her forward. "There's someone you must meet."

"Yes. I should think so," she says with a huge grin.

"Dam, this is my mate, Aine, my amavi compar," he says, his eyes sparkling and full of pride. "Amavi, this is my dam, Li'andra."

"You are so lovely," she says, letting go of Griz and wrapping me in a warm embrace.

It reminds me of the hugs I used to get from my mum, and try as I might, the waterworks come on again.

"Isn't my youngling's mate beautiful?" she asks his Aunt Felina.

"She is," her sister agrees. "Hair the color of Packari

sands."

"Thank you," I sniffle, trying not to leak snot in her hair.

Li'andra hugs me again. "I have so looked forward to meeting you, my darling. And, now, I can't wait to meet this one!"

She presses her hand to my belly, setting off a blush that I can feel heating my entire face.

"You certainly didn't waste any time, Griz," Horok teases.

"I hear you didn't, either." Griz grins back. "At least, I'm only shooting for one at a time."

Everyone laughs except me. It's kind of uncomfortable being the only person crying, but with my hormones so out of control with the pregnancy, there's simply no help for it. I cry when I'm happy, I cry when I'm sad. Hell, I cry all the time. Wiping my tears with the back of my hand, I smile and try to get through the next round of introductions.

"Oh! Let me introduce my father," I tell them, grabbing Bruce and dragging him between me and Griz. "This is Bruce MacTavish."

Griz's mother looks up, the happy smile on her face slowly fading, replaced with something else as she looks at him oddly. Crap. I've seen that look before.

In fact, I saw that look just this morning before I ever got out of bed. From her son!

I turn around to look at Bruce, only to find that he, too, has the same flustered, doe-eyed look aimed at Griz's mom. As I feared, when I slide my gaze to Griz, he's scowling daggers at Bruce.

Well, shit.

"Nice to meet you, Li'andra," Bruce purrs her name like a jungle cat.

"Likewise," she coos, peeking at Bruce from beneath her long, blonde lashes. Now, Griz's eye has started to tic.

"Bruce is going to be taking an engineering position onboard our friend Epherus' ship," Griz informs her, slapping his hand on Epherus' shoulder and shoving him in front of Bruce. "I doubt he'll be around much."

My jaw drops open. Actually drops open, hits the floor like one of those cartoon characters on television. By the time I close it, Bruce speaks up.

"Maybe, maybe not," he chuffs, elbowing his way past Epherus and snaking his arm around Li'andra's shoulders. "I kinda like the looks of this place. Did I hear there was a spread around here where a hungry man could get a bite to eat?" he asks her.

Griz's hands begin to fist, and Epherus, no surprise, laughs so hard, his blue face turns red.

"What's so funny, Epherus?" Griz growls.

"Call me Eff," he chokes out as he falls in behind Bruce and Li'andra.

"Let's all go," Horok says. "We've prepared a feast to celebrate your return and your recent mating. Aine, your friends Jill and Celia are waiting for us there. This way."

Tingling with excitement, I nearly take off skipping, except I'm pregnant and I really can't. Still, I'm ecstatic to see Jill and Celia again. Celia's been in the hospital, along with Epherus' sister, and was only released a few days ago.

"Ready?" Griz asks, still a little peeved.

I slide my arms around my mate's waist and pull him in for a hug. He looks down at me, and I give him my best smile. It's not difficult to do. I can't remember ever being happier.

"I love you," I tell him, and the last trace of anger in his eyes fades away, leaving behind only warmth and affection.

"I love you, too, amavi." He hugs me tighter leaning down to press his lips to mine.

And all thoughts of Kings and Queens, close friends, and mischievous parents melt away.

# EPILOGUE

Epherus

Stepping inside the new hospital wing, it occurs to me that I've spent more time here on Tarilax these past couple of cycles than I have on Aurelia IV in the entire past rotation. Goddess knows, I have plenty of work to do. I should be on Vilox with my comrades killing Borgks right now. Or, on Shalmot, cashing in on an easy contract by disposing of that dirty politician, Galex Tristavi. But, something here keeps pulling me back.

Haelic. Just admit it. Some*one* keeps pulling me back. It's that female, that damn human female, the tall one with legs like an Amazon and curves that make my cock twitch. She may be tall compared to the other human females, but she's a delicate, little flower to me, one whose scent drives me insane. And those long, brown curls of hers seem to haunt my dreams. I long to plunge my hand in them, wrap them around my fist as I pound into that luscious behind.

"Grr."

Shiest. Now, I'm growling at myself.

Ever since I saw her training with that Tarilean warrior, Nordric, I can't get her out of my mind. The way she flipped him over her shoulder and nailed him to the mat, using those long, smooth legs of hers to hold him immobile nearly drove me crazy. It was the sexiest frizzucking thing I've seen in my entire life. I get hard every time I think about it. I wanted to volunteer to train with her next, just to pin her beneath me.

I reach the room number the nurse gave me and glance down as my hand rests on the doorknob. Just frizzucking great. I can't go in there with a tent in my pants.

I stand there for a few clicks waiting for the swelling to go down, trying not to think about the brown-haired siren, and failing miserably. Horok calls them his goddesses, the human females. I don't know about the rest of them, but I call mine my beautiful Amazon.

Laughter floats through tiny cracks in the closed door, and the sound of that human male's voice makes me smile. He has an odd name, Bruce, but I like him. That in itself is odd because I don't like many people. Then again, there aren't too many people as funny as he is. When we first met, I would have laid odds that he and his new son-in-law would have killed each other by now, but surprisingly, they seem to be getting along. Maybe because Griz's mate threatened to ship them both off with me to Aurelia IV if they didn't straighten up. Too bad Bruce didn't accept my job offer. I could have used the comic relief. He's not too bad of an engineer, either.

One final peek at my zipper tells me I've dallied here long enough. Swinging open the door, I duck my head and enter. The doorways in this place are just like all the others, not tall enough to accommodate my height. Haelic, they're barely wide enough to fit the girth of my shoulders.

"Eff!" Griz's mate looks good, quite healthy for someone who's just given birth to a thirteen stone, half-grown youngling.

"Hello, female." I lean over and pat her on head. She's not so bad as females go. "You look well."

"I am." She beams. "Have you come to see the baby?"

*No. I've come to see Lisa.* "Yes. Of course."

"Well, you're in luck. I just fed him, and he's still awake. You'll have to pry him away from Lisa, though." She blinks one eye at me as she often does whenever she mentions my

Amazon.

"Is there something wrong with your eye?" Good thing she's already in a hospital where they can take a look at it for her.

She huffs and frowns at me. "No. My eye's fine."

"Eff! Come to see my new grandson, eh, bramair?"

I look up to see Bruce, his arm wrapped protectively around Griz's dam as they talk to Aine's flaming-haired doctor, Maggie.

I nod at him, unable to keep the silly smile off my face. At first, I thought he was only flirting with Li'andra to irritate Griz, but he seems honestly smitten with the female. The feeling looks to be mutual, too, from the way she's snuggling into him.

"Hey, Eff." Griz smiles as he plops down on the bed next to his mate and gives her a kiss.

As usual, those two can't seem to keep their hands, or their lips, off one another. I suspect we'll all be here again in a few cycles looking at another youngling.

"Griz." I give him a quick nod.

"How's your sister?"

My sister. Poor, sweet female. I really want to kill that dirty lizard, Beahl, but he's been under the protection of the Tarilean justice system. As if that could really stop me. For once, I'm giving the judicial system a chance to work. Beahl and his entire crew will go to trial next cycle, and when that's over, there are three other planets who want to try them. I must attempt to be satisfied with that. I probably will be, unless his final sentence is anything less than death. Then, I'll have to take matters into my own hands.

"My sister is doing much better. I left her on Aurelia IV with our family, and they are focusing on her recovery."

"That's good. Really good," he says, turning to his mate and picking up a lock of her bright red hair. He rubs it absently between his fingers as he smiles at her. "Amavi, Jill and Celia just com'd. They're on their way here to see the youngling."

"Oh, wonderful!" she chirps, her face lighting up. "Eff has to meet him first, though." She cranes her neck, looking around the crowded room. "Hey, Lisa! Bring the baby over so I can introduce him to Eff."

My hearts race, and I feel a little dizzy as I turn to see my beautiful Amazon striding toward me with a tiny youngling in her arms.

*Mine! My mate!*

What the frizzuck? Where did that come from? I give my head a shake and frown at the unwelcome thought. What would I do with a mate?

"I'm not real sure if we should introduce them or not. The look on Eff's face will probably give the sweet little thing nightmares." She laughs, her eyes sparkling with mischief.

Goddess, but she's breathtaking.

"Here," she says, holding the youngling toward me. "You want to hold him?"

Haelic, no! If I sneezed, I might blow the tiny thing out of my hand. I manage to shake my head without seeming too unfriendly, I think.

"Well, that's okay," she says, sidling up close beside me so she can show it to me. Stars, I want to kiss her.

"Eff, meet Bruce Grizolde Theodosius Ja'Lento," she says, pulling the tiny blanket back so I can see the youngling's face.

We stare at each other for a moment, sizing one another up, and then, he belches. Yes, he'll make a fine macki some day. I smile and show him my fangs.

"Holy shit," Lisa says almost in a whisper. Just as I turn my head to look at her, she pokes her little finger between my lips and glides it over my fang. "That's impressive."

Holy frizzuck! My cock gets hard so fast, I nearly pass out from the blood loss to my head. I feel my eyes begin to glaze with undiluted lust, and it takes everything in me not to sling her over my shoulder and take off with her. If she weren't holding Griz's youngling, I would.

She knows nothing about Aurelian mating, the sensitivity of our fangs and horns, our instincts to dominate, our need to subdue and control our females. It would take a lot of time and effort to train her properly. I feel a slow smile creeping across my lips. I think I'm going to enjoy this.

"Eff, will you be staying long this time?" Griz's mate asks casually.

I tear my attention away from the sexy little Amazon and make an attempt to be polite.

"No."

She stares at me expectantly and finally rolls her eyes. "Well, how long are you staying?"

"I have to leave tomorrow tonight," I tell her. "I just hired a new engineer, and we have a job lined up."

She looks relieved. I get the feeling she wasn't too happy that I initially offered the job to Bruce. Aine glances at my Amazon and then cuts her eyes back to me and smirks. "And, when are you coming back?"

"Depends."

"On?" Lisa asks, and I turn to look at her, surprised that she would even care.

Should I dare get my hopes up? Is she really interested in when I'll be back? Could she want me to come back soon? I notice everyone staring at me, and I remember she asked me a question.

"Depends on how well the new guy does. He's a human," I say, summing up my concerns in one word. "I would never have considered hiring another human, but he reminds me of Bruce."

"A human? Really? You'll have to bring him by for dinner when you get back. I can invite Lisa, too." She smiles wryly, and I notice Griz gently shaking his head at her. "And, Bruce and Li'andra, and others, too," she quickly amends.

"Count us in," Bruce shouts. "I'd never turn down good, free scran."

"I'll think about it," I reply begrudgingly. I'd much rather have my Amazon all to myself. "I'm not sure Lachlin is one for dinner parties."

Suddenly, Griz's mate screams and jumps straight up in her bed. Bruce shoves Li'andra at Griz and staggers forward, his face pale and ashy.

"Lachlin?" They both say at the same time.

The End . . . For now

# ABOUT THE AUTHOR

Wife, mother, and avid animal lover, D. Morrissey was born and raised in small-town Arkansas, just a stone's throw away from Little Rock. A business executive by day, she spends most of her nights penning steamy romance novels. While her books cover various genres from contemporary mystery to sci-fi fantasy, you will find the prevailing themes through all include smart, funny females and hot, loyal males. Her list of credits includes Rhone, His Goddess, His Warrior Princess, His Sexy Duchess, Insanity Plea, Just Plain Crazy, All That Sparkles, Liar, and Deceiver.